As the director patt  **heard footsteps app** **turning, she knew i**

He was smiling, and so her brain scrambling and goose bumps rushing across her arms.

"Morning, Director," he said when he was still a couple of paces away. Then he turned his dark, somehow mischievous gaze on Gen, and she froze.

"Morning, Zach…"

The director's words trailed away as Zach paused and, bending his head, kissed Gen on her cheek, leaving a warm, electrically charged spot on her skin.

"Morning, love," he murmured, and Gen swore she heard barely suppressed laughter in his deep, soft tone. "Sleep well?"

"Y-yes, thank you" was all she could get out past the lump of mingled horror and laughter clogging her throat. "You?"

"Never better," he replied.

Then he strolled away, as casual as could be, leaving Gen biting the inside of her cheek, hardly daring to look at Director Hamilton. Then she heard the wail of an approaching ambulance and shook her head, pushing all of it aside as she hurried toward emerge.

She'd deal with Zachary Lewin later. Oh, yes, she would.

Dear Reader,

Welcome back to the fictional Caribbean island of St. Eustace, where fun in the sun and sexy romance awaits!

Anyone who knows me knows I love island life. It's not all rum punch or what you see in vacation advertisements, but usually there's a more laid-back vibe that calls to you to take things at a slower pace. To meet with friends, go to eat or dance at an out-of-the-way venue, to leave city life for the diverse landscapes of the country or to hang out at the beach.

In *Island Fling with the Surgeon*, Gen and Zach, two people running away from their urban existence—and past problems—find themselves caught up in the most unlikely affair. It starts out as a lark and ends up causing a seismic shift in their lives, all against the backdrop of secrets, family drama and sultry tropical days…and nights.

Distrustful and hurt by their last relationships, they set out on an adventure in deception that could lead them to happiness…or destroy their newfound friendship.

Read on to find out what happens, and I hope you're swept away by another trip to St. Eustace (first introduced in *Best Friend to Doctor Right*).

Ann McIntosh

ISLAND FLING
WITH THE SURGEON

———

ANN McINTOSH

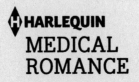

HARLEQUIN

MEDICAL
ROMANCE

HARLEQUIN®
MEDICAL
ROMANCE™

Recycling programs
for this product may
not exist in your area.

ISBN-13: 978-1-335-40871-6

Island Fling with the Surgeon

Copyright © 2021 by Ann McIntosh

All rights reserved. No part of this book may be used or reproduced in
any manner whatsoever without written permission except in the case of
brief quotations embodied in critical articles and reviews.

This is a work of fiction. Names, characters, places and incidents
are either the product of the author's imagination or are used fictitiously.
Any resemblance to actual persons, living or dead, businesses,
companies, events or locales is entirely coincidental.

This edition published by arrangement with Harlequin Books S.A.

For questions and comments about the quality of this book,
please contact us at CustomerService@Harlequin.com.

Harlequin Enterprises ULC
22 Adelaide St. West, 40th Floor
Toronto, Ontario M5H 4E3, Canada
www.Harlequin.com

Printed in U.S.A.

Ann McIntosh was born in the tropics, lived in the frozen north for a number of years and now resides in sunny central Florida with her husband. She's a proud mama to three grown children, loves tea, crafting, animals (except reptiles!), bacon and the ocean. She believes in the power of romance to heal, inspire and provide hope in our complex world.

Books by Ann McIntosh

Harlequin Medical Romance

A Summer in São Paulo

Awakened by Her Brooding Brazilian

The Nurse's Pregnancy Miracle
The Surgeon's One Night to Forever
Surgeon Prince, Cinderella Bride
The Nurse's Christmas Temptation
Best Friend to Doctor Right
Christmas with Her Lost-and-Found Lover
Night Shifts with the Miami Doc

Visit the Author Profile page at Harlequin.com.

Dedicated to my longtime friends Renee, Odette and June. Good fren betta dan pocket money. Miss yuh, and mi soon come!

CHAPTER ONE

THE FIRST TIME Dr. Genevieve Broussard operated with the assistance of surgical nurse Zachary Lewin she was cautious, as was normal when working with new personnel. But the main difference, in that circumstance, was how aware she was of him. His presence alone put her on high alert in a way she didn't imagine she'd be if he were a woman.

Of course, it was hard *not* to be aware of Zach. Although he wasn't exceptionally tall—perhaps three or four inches above her own five foot six—he was barrel-chested and solid; the muscles in his arms and legs seemed set to tear open the seams of his scrubs.

He was also very good-looking, his skin the color of café au lait with a sprinkle of light freckles across his nose and cheeks, making her wonder if he had any elsewhere. Not conventionally handsome by any means, but striking in a serious, no-nonsense type of way. The lovely British accent didn't hurt either, adding a rather exotic flair to an already interesting package.

And he had a direct, interrogative way of looking at her, as though his dark brown gaze was trying to ferret out her every secret.

He was also quiet and—she later came to learn—rather solitary, with an air of distance that forestalled any impertinence or overtures of friendship.

Not that, at the time, she was considering fostering any kind of camaraderie. She hadn't come to St. Eustace to make friends, especially of the male persuasion. All she needed to know was whether he was competent in the operating room or not. Especially since the anesthesiologist she'd been assigned was one of the new doctors who'd traveled to St. Eustace to gain extra experience.

She'd been assured the young anesthesiologist was capable, and all she had to do was keep an eye on him and write a report afterward, but the teenage patient on her operation table was her first concern. Kingston Matthews had been stuck by a car in downtown Port Michael and suffered life-threatening internal injuries. As trauma surgeon on duty when he came in, Gen had gotten him into the operating room as quickly as possible.

He'd needed a partial splenectomy, and ahead lay the surgical splinting of a couple of severely fractured ribs, but that had to wait until she was able to stop all the internal bleeding.

"Suction," she said, realizing as the word left her lips that the tube was already almost in place, Zach anticipating her request.

Blood trickled back into view.

She waited for an update on BP and O-sat from the anesthesiologist, as she carefully retracted the exposed organs, looking for the bleeder, but it was Zach who supplied the information.

Glancing up, Gen was just in time to see the anesthesiologist give the nurse a glare, but when he glanced her way and she raised her brows, all the doctor did was look away.

Even being very new—to the hospital, and to his duties—she'd expected better. This called for a talk with him later, to make sure he recognized the importance of communicating necessary information.

Kingston Matthews's blood pressure had risen since the splenectomy and the repair to a damaged minor artery, but it still wasn't up to where it should be. And wouldn't get there until she found the other bleed.

She'd already checked the liver and stomach

for damage, surprisingly not finding any, but maybe she'd missed something?

The suction tube appeared again and, as she watched, Zach moved it slowly, clearing away the blood and revealing where the first trickle reappeared.

It was at that point she realized the extent of his experience and knowledge.

There were some surgical nurses who actively, if unobtrusively, used know-how gained over many years to be a surgeon's other pair of eyes and hands.

Some surgeons pretended it didn't happen, or feigned being oblivious, but Gen wasn't one of them. When the life of the patient was on the line, she'd take every advantage she could get to keep them alive, and be grateful.

"Thank you," she said. "I see it."

As she was about to cauterize the small blood vessel, the vision in her left eye blurred slightly.

Dammit.

She was usually more aware of when her eye was becoming dry, but she'd been so intent on finding the source of the bleeding, she'd left the mitigating exercise too long.

Her eye problem was a lasting effect of the Bell's palsy she'd suffered just after qualifying as a surgeon, causing the lid to noticeably droop. Unfortunately, the nerve damage also meant that her left eye didn't blink as efficiently as the right. At first, she'd been terrified that it would scotch her career, especially when it became clear she'd never fully recover, but over time she'd learned how to live with it and still operate.

"One second," she said, using the muscles above her eyebrow to force the offending eye closed, allowing lacrimal fluid to lubricate the eyeball. At any other time, she'd have simply used her finger to manipulate the eyelid, but she'd had to develop a different method of dealing with it when at work.

Especially in the sterile environment of the operating room.

After getting her eye open, she looked up, blinking to make sure her vision was clear, and caught Zach watching her.

In the past, it would have made her angry, or exacerbated the embarrassment that had followed her for a long time. Even now, she felt a rush of heat rise into her face, but she lifted her chin, daring him to say anything.

But those dark eyes just surveyed her, seemingly impassive and infinitely patient.

When she was studying, one of her instructors had told the class, "A surgeon must exhibit complete confidence at all times. You're like the captain of a ship. Everyone is looking to you to steer through the rocks and make safe harbor."

Bearing that in mind, she said briskly, "Okay. Here we go." She heard the defensiveness in her own voice, but hoped no one else did.

Zach simply nodded, but before he turned his attention back to the patient, she thought she'd seen a flash of something in his eyes, although she wasn't sure what it was.

All she knew was that it filled her with a different kind of warmth. One that had lasted the rest of the successful operation and even carried over for a couple of days.

Now, five months later, as she sat in the doctor's lounge with her fingers pushed into her hair, distractedly pulling at the short strands, she was sure it was then she'd told her mother the whopper.

The biggest, silliest lie of her life, which now had her contemplating whether it was too late to apply for another job.

Maybe in Nepal, or somewhere like that?

Far, far away.

Too far for her mother to fly to from New Orleans.

"Coo-calloo-calloo," she muttered to herself, using the expression she'd made up when she was eight, right after her father washed her mouth out with soap for cursing.

"What was that?"

The amused question from the doorway had Gen straightening to see orthopedic surgeon Mina Haraldson coming into the room. The grin on the other woman's face had Gen smiling too, although she felt anything but amused by her predicament.

"It's the strongest curse word I know. I made it up myself, so I could use it in front of my parents and not get in trouble," she admitted, making Mina laugh.

"Now, what on earth has you cursing so horribly?" the other woman asked, once she'd stopped chuckling.

Even though she liked Mina, and they'd developed a nice rapport, Gen hesitated. After what had happened with her so-called best friend, Loren, she'd gotten out of the habit of confiding in others.

Not that she expected everyone in her life to be a backstabber, but the experience, although occurring years before, had left her cautious.

So instead, as she watched Mina pour herself a cup of coffee, she asked, "Is that a new prosthesis?"

Mina shot her a sideways glance, before looking back to reach for the creamer. "Yes. Arrived two days ago. I'm still getting used to it, but I have to admit it's pretty badass."

They'd spoken about Mina's accident, when she'd lost her hand, and her previous resistance to getting a prosthesis. It had seemed a waste of time getting one, she said, when it wouldn't enable her to operate on patients. But eventually she'd come around, realizing she could do so much more with one. And, once the prosthetic company she'd approached about making the hand for her realized the possibilities, they'd asked her to become one of their main testers.

"It looks it," Gen replied, admiring the realistic appearance and the movement of the fingers as Mina picked up her cup with it, while stirring the coffee with her right.

As she walked over to the table and sat across from Gen, Mina replied, "The action is unbelievably smooth. Almost as smooth as that change of subject you just did."

Gen couldn't help the little groan that escaped her throat, even though the other woman's comment made her smile too.

"Clearly not smooth enough," she replied, letting amusement color her words.

Mina held up her hand. "Hey, I'm not trying to pry, but you sounded pretty upset. I'm here, if you need an ear."

She was smiling as she spoke, but Gen saw how serious Mina's eyes were, and a pang of loneliness made her chest ache. Suddenly, she went from reticent to wanting to tell the other woman the whole sorry story.

Hopefully, Mina wouldn't think her nuts.

"My younger sister called to warn me that Mom is planning to come to St. Eustace in a couple of weeks to surprise me."

Mina's gaze sharpened. "Warn you?"

Something in her tone had Gen hurrying to continue, not wanting to give the wrong impression.

"Mom's amazing, and I can't wait to see her, but..." She realized she was pressing the knuckle of her index finger into the numb space at the left-hand corner of her lips, and forced herself to stop.

Mina took a sip of her coffee, obviously giving Gen a chance to continue. When the silence stretched on, she said, "But?"

Embarrassed, Gen dropped her chin to her chest for a moment, then sighed as heat rose into her cheeks.

Best to just get it over with.

"I went through a rough patch after I got sick, and it threw Mom into hyper-nurture mode, and she hasn't come out of it since. It's really only seemed to get worse once I decided to come to St. Eustace."

She shook her head, not wanting to go into details about the Bell's palsy, and her then-fiancé's painful defection, which Gen would be the first to admit she hadn't handled very well. And now how hard it was, knowing her mother was fretting about Gen's mental and emotional health, and that she was too far away to do anything, should her daughter need her.

Meeting Mina's sympathetic gaze gave her the impetus to continue.

"Mom's hell-bent on my going back to New Orleans. She seems to think I'm here hiding, not getting on with what she calls my 'real life.' So, I spontaneously came up with an idea to make her feel I was having a great time here and was extremely happy."

"Oh?" Mina's eyebrows went up. "What did you tell her?"

Taking a deep breath, Gen replied on a rushed exhale, "That I was seeing someone. Then, to make it worse, I built an elaborate fantasy about the guy and our relationship."

"Uh-oh." Mina put her cup on the table and actually leaned forward, as though in anticipation. "What are you going to do?"

"I don't know." She tried to sound adult, but the ridiculousness of it was hard to ignore. "It sounds so juvenile when I say it out loud—like when a teenager tells their friends they do so have a boyfriend, but he goes to a different school."

Mina's eyes were wide as she said, "Yeah, but that's when you're a kid and you lie to your friends. This is your mom, and if she's anything like mine, heads could roll."

"Tell me about it," Gen said, the words coming out more like a groan. "She'll kill me if she finds out."

"If?" The skepticism in Mina's voice was unmistakable. "How could she not?"

Gen just dropped her head back into her hand, unwilling to answer the question, or even tell Mina the rest of the story.

She hadn't just told her mother she was seeing *someone*; she'd said she was seeing Zachary Lewin.

Named him, specifically.

And Marielle Broussard was no shrinking violet. Even if Gen told her the relationship hadn't worked out, she'd want to know why. And she'd be on the lookout for the man in question the entire time she was on St. Eustace, inclined to glare, or outright ask what had gone wrong.

Not to mention, Gen would be right back where she started, with her mother all up in her business and pushing for her to go back to the States.

"I have two choices," she muttered toward the floor. "Pretend to have broken up with the man, or set up a fake relationship well enough to fool my mother."

Mina blew out a breath, then asked, "What was that word you used, when I walked into the room?"

"Coo-calloo-calloo."

"Yeah," Mina replied in a rueful tone. "Coo-calloo-calloo."

Zach Lewin closed his locker, then snapped the padlock into place, but instead of heading straight out the door as he usually would, he stood there a little longer, lost in thought.

Normally he easily compartmentalized work, and once he was finished a shift rarely let his thoughts stray back to anything to do with the hospital. But today was different, and it wasn't a patient he was worried about, but one of the surgeons.

Dr. Genevieve Broussard.

They'd worked together earlier in the day, operating on a patient who'd come in with volvulus. While Dr. Broussard had performed with her usual calm competence, Zach was sure he sensed a difference in the way she'd spoken and behaved toward him. A certain coolness that hadn't been present the umpteen other times they'd worked together.

He wasn't given to flights of fancy. In fact,

he'd been described as unimaginative and detached. If memory served, *daft* and *oblivious* had been tossed about too, but who was counting? Yet, he was sure he'd sensed something strange in Dr. Broussard's manner during and after the operation.

And it irked him.

He admired her skill as a surgeon. They'd always got on well, and had a cordial relationship. She had an effervescent personality, although mixed with firm professionalism. It was a combination that worked well for her, as he hadn't heard one murmur of complaint about her the entire time he'd been at the hospital. She seemed universally liked and never appeared to have any problems with anyone, which made her change in attitude toward him all the more noticeable.

Normally he'd brush it off and leave it alone. His time in the military and as a nurse had taught him not to expect everyone to like him and, if someone didn't, not to take it to heart or even care. But the sudden shift in their previously easy working relationship gave him pause, and made him want to know if it was because of something he'd done. If he'd inadvertently caused the change, it made complete sense to make it right, since they'd be working together for at least the foreseeable future.

Another thing he'd learned was to nip problems that had the potential to become career threatening in the bud. While unsure whether this could be classified that way or not, he wasn't willing to take the chance.

He'd come to St. Eustace to get away for a while and get his head on straight. Although he didn't plan on staying forever, this was, after all, his father's homeland, and he wanted to maintain the family's good name while he was here.

Yet, did it make sense to bring it up at all, at this early stage? Maybe she'd just been having a bad day, and he'd presented an easy target?

He bent to pick up his kit bag, still unsure of what to do but leaning toward letting things remain as they were, just to see what would happen when next they worked together. That wouldn't be for at least three days, what with their overlapping days off.

Right, then.

Decision made, Zach headed out of the changing room, only to see the object of his ruminations standing just down the hall, looking at her phone. She was still in her scrubs, but her bag was on the bench next to her, and he knew from the schedule that, barring emergencies, she was now off duty.

So, why was she hanging about?

And, even with the decision he'd only just

made, he was tempted to stop and speak to her about what had happened earlier. In fact, he found himself heading right toward her, but before he'd taken more than two strides, a door on his right opened and Dr. Kiah Langdon stepped out.

Kiah immediately stopped and said, "Hey, cuz. On your way to the gym?"

From the corner of his eye Zach saw Dr. Broussard turn her head toward them, before he gave his full attention to Kiah.

"Going down to Coconut Beach for a run," he replied.

"How's the house coming?"

Kiah knew Zach was refurbishing his grandfather's home, which had sat mostly empty since the old man died, and always took a moment to ask about the progress being made.

"Good. Finished the veranda and just about to start upgrading the kitchen."

And by the time they'd finished chatting, Genevieve Broussard was gone, leaving him no option but to revert to his prior plan of letting things ride and seeing what would happen.

The drive over to Coconut Beach took only about fifteen minutes, but Zach found his thoughts repeatedly going back to Genevieve, no matter how he tried to keep them on other matters. So much so that, on turning into the car park next to the beach, he thought perhaps his eyes, following the lead of his brain, were playing tricks on him.

That couldn't be Dr. Broussard sitting on the bonnet of her car waving to him, as he pulled into a nearby space, could it?

It most certainly was, and as she hopped down from her perch and made her way toward his car, bemusement had the muscles in his neck tightening.

What the heck was going on?

He had hardly closed the car door behind him before she started speaking.

"Hey, I'm sorry to stalk you like this, but I really needed to talk to you, and the hospital wasn't the best place to do it..."

Although she stopped to take a breath, Zach didn't have a chance to utter even one word before she asked, "Would you be my boyfriend?"

CHAPTER TWO

GEN HADN'T MEANT to blurt it out like that, but she was so nervous her palms were sweating, her knees were weak and the words just tumbled out of her mouth. The look of shock on Zach's face just made it all worse. Heat climbed the back of her neck, and she rubbed at it, trying to dispel the prickling sensation.

"I'm sorry?" he said, his voice clipped and terribly precise, sharp enough to cut. "I beg your pardon?"

"Oof," she replied, then wished she could pull the inarticulate sound back into her mouth, especially when his eyebrows contracted into a fierce scowl. Who would have thought she'd won prizes for elocution in the past, if that was the best she could come up with? "No, *I'm* sorry. I know it sounds crazy, but will you give me a chance to explain?"

He was still wearing that scowl, and the searching nature of his gaze made her wonder if he thought she was nuts.

She was wondering the same thing herself and couldn't blame him if he were!

"I'm waiting with bated breath for you to do just that," he said with a hint of sarcasm overlaying the words.

She rubbed at her nape again and tried to regain some hint of composure.

"I'm not propositioning you, although I know it sounds like it." The urge to start babbling again had her stopping and taking a deep breath. After blowing it out, she continued. "The truth is, I lied to my mother and told her you and I were involved in a relationship."

"You *what*?"

He said it softly, but he couldn't have sounded any more dangerous if he'd shouted.

Gen held up her hands. "I know. I know. It was stupid, but Mom is always on at me about not having a social life, and one night I just couldn't take it anymore. So, I made up a story to get her off my back."

Not the entire truth, but close enough under the circumstances.

"Why me?"

Now she could hear curiosity warring with

his outrage, and it made her embarrassment deepen, if that were at all possible.

"I don't know for sure," she replied, trying to be honest. "I think it was because you'd just arrived, and I'd worked with you in the OR for the first time, so your name just popped into my head."

Zach shook his head slowly, still giving her a suspicious glare.

"And now—?"

"Now Mom's coming to visit, and I can't let her know I lied."

His nostrils flared slightly, as he drew in a harsh breath. "Just tell her it didn't work out, and we're not friendly anymore. Wouldn't that solve the problem?"

"No!" Yikes, now she was barking at him. She had to get a grip. "It would make it worse—for me anyway—because then the whole cycle would start again."

His gaze made her feel like a recalcitrant child, and now her entire body flushed hot. Looking around, she spied a small gazebo farther along the beach and gestured toward it.

"Can we sit down and talk about it?" Yeah, she was pleading, but although it felt weird, she was willing to do whatever it took to get Zach on board with her plan, no matter how crazy it was.

He didn't reply for such a long interval she was absolutely sure he was going to tell her to get lost, but finally he nodded and waved his hand in the direction of the hut.

"After you."

"Thank you," she said as they started walking that way. "I really appreciate it."

"Don't thank me yet," he said in that cool, cutting tone. "I haven't agreed to anything."

"You agreed to at least hear me out," she pointed out, perhaps more sharply than she should, all things considered.

That earned her a stern, sidelong glance, but he was gracious enough to say, "That's fair."

By the time they sat across from each other at the shaded table, she was struggling with what she was going to say. It had sounded, if not sensible, at least reasonable when she'd rehearsed it all in her head, but now all that she'd planned to say fled in the face of that interrogatory gaze.

"Well?" he said, not breaking eye contact. "What do you have to say for yourself?"

She was suddenly catapulted back in time to the principal's office, where she was supposed to explain how one of her many escapades had gone awry and the sensations were still the same.

Embarrassment.

Shame.

But also the unmistakable high of an adventure unfolding.

The last made her smile, and Zach's scowl grew even more ferocious.

"The fact is," she started quickly, before he could cuss her out the way he seemed set to do. "My mother thinks that I'm suffering ongoing psychological effects from my bout of Bell's, and I'm trying my hardest to reassure her that isn't the case."

"Are you sure you aren't, though?" he asked, no longer looking as fierce as he had a moment before.

"No." She shook her head in emphasis. "I'll freely admit it was a setback I wasn't anticipating—not that anyone anticipates a situation like that—but my main concern, really, was whether it was going to destroy my career. Once I got to the stage where I knew I could still operate, I was okay with what had happened."

Again, not the full story, but enough for him to get the gist without exposing her private issues too much.

He looked skeptical, but only said, "So, if you're okay, why the deception? Wouldn't it be better to just tell your mother the truth, instead of lying to her?"

"I've tried repeatedly, believe me, but she's unrelenting." Gen rubbed at her eye, which was getting a little dry, but stopped when Zach's gaze followed the motion of her finger. She quickly continued, "I know she just wants to see me happy, but the stress of her constant worrying was wearing me out. Telling her I was in a relationship at least allayed some of her fears."

Zach pondered her words in silence, and Gen wondered what was going on in his head. There was more to it, of course, but she wasn't willing to tell him about Johan abandoning her after the Bell's palsy, or the shock of him marrying Loren immediately thereafter. The aftereffects of her illness were nothing in comparison to the pain of the betrayal. If anything was holding her back from moving forward in life and considering getting involved with a man again, it was that.

"So, what exactly did you tell your mother about our imaginary relationship?"

Gen gave him her most winning smile, aware that it was a lot more lopsided than it had been when she used it on her teachers, parents and any others she wanted to impress. Hopefully it would still do the trick.

"I told her that you're fabulously good-looking and had a body to die for. And, because my mom is big on excellence, I also told her you're the best surgical nurse I've ever worked with."

His lips twitched, ever so slightly, at the corners.

"In other words, you've compounded the original lie several times over."

She wrinkled her nose and shook her head. "Not one of those statements is a lie. You are extremely handsome, and you obviously work hard to stay fit, so I don't know why you wouldn't just admit your body is amazing. Plus, you actually are one of the best, if not *the* best surgical nurse I've had in the operating room."

He gave what could only be classified as a snort and said, "Now I know you're just buttering me up. What else did you tell her?"

His modesty made her smile. Who knew that humbleness could be so attractive and tempting? His brushing aside her honest compliments made her want to push, to see what it would take to make him really self-conscious.

"I told her your father was originally from St. Eustace, but you were born in England and had a sexy English accent." She paused, thinking back to the conversations she'd had with her mother, then added, "And that although you're ridiculously cute, you're not flashy in any way."

He rubbed the side of his hand across his lips, and Gen saw a little rush of color stain his cheeks for an instant.

"Good grief. I meant, what did you tell her about the progress of this mythical relationship of ours? Such as, what we were supposedly doing over the last few months? Have we got serious or anything ridiculous like that?"

For some reason, hearing him talk about them getting serious as "ridiculous" kinda hurt. Was there something about her that made him think her unfit to be serious girlfriend, or even wife, material?

Realizing she was pushing at the corner of her mouth, she dropped her hand back onto the table and replied, "Well, I told her you were getting over a really bad breakup and weren't interested in getting too involved too soon, and that slowed her down some."

His demeanor changed so quickly it was shocking, going from slightly amused to cold and intense in a blink.

"Who told you that?"

There was that soft, dangerous voice again, coupled with a narrow-eyed stare. It should have sent alarm bells ringing like crazy, but instead Gen felt a tingle of unmistakable excitement rush through her veins.

"No one told me anything," she replied, trying for a conciliatory tone and wondering if she'd touched a nerve. "I made it up, remember?"

His response was to swing his leg over the bench and get up so abruptly she was left looking up at him, bemused.

"Listen, this is just bonkers," he said. Pausing, he rubbed a hand across his mouth again. "I can't even digest this right now. I'm going for a run. If you're here when I get back, I'll try again to listen to what you have to say, but I can't right now."

Then he took off at a blistering pace, leaving her with a mouthwatering view of a whole lot of hard-bodied man in motion.

As she watched his long muscular legs and amazing butt disappear along the shoreline, Gen shook her head, wondering why her heart was pounding so hard. And she couldn't help asking herself if it was worth waiting for him to come back. Who knew how long he'd be, or if he'd have run off the snarky attitude?

Getting up, she picked up her car keys, then just stood there, stupidly poised between staying and going, unable to make up her mind about what to do.

Looking to where Zach was just disappearing around a bluff was like watching her grand, brilliant plan disappear into the sunset.

"Coo-calloo-calloo," she muttered. "Coo-calloo-ca-cock-a-doodle-do."

Zach pushed himself hard for the first two hundred meters of his run, then, when his muscles started reminding him that he hadn't done his usual warm-up routine, he slowed.

It felt, strangely enough, as though he was running for his life, from a woman who was in turns amusing, infuriating and—curiously—beguiling. He'd seen Gen Broussard in work mode, but hadn't spent much time in casual conversation with her, so he hadn't known what it would be like to be the recipient of her full attention. Or that she had all the impish charm of a pixie.

Those dark twinkling eyes that seemed to be perpetually laughing at herself and the world, coupled with her beautiful, asymmetrical grin, had made it hard for him to truly take in what she was saying.

What she was asking of him.

And when she said she'd told her mother he'd had a bad breakup, he'd been shocked. So much so that the hurt, which he'd assiduously pushed to the back of his mind, was as sharp as the day his very real relationship imploded. The wave of embarrassment that had inundated him almost knocked him off his seat and made him wonder if the entire island knew his sorry story.

Hence the quick retreat, which he refused to think of as running away, although clearly it rather was.

She'd said she'd made it up so, clearly, she hadn't actually heard how he'd been used by Moira, then discarded like a piece of chewed gum. Now, remembering the honesty he'd heard in her tone filled him with relief. He'd come to the island to get away from the embarrassment, and the thought of once again being the recipient of pity, sympathy or unkind amusement made him cringe.

That aside, even now he found it impossible to believe Genevieve had told her mother they were involved. If an hour ago someone had asked him to describe Dr. Broussard, he'd have used words like sensible, and steady. That was her persona in the hospital, and definitely when she was in the operating theater, so this whole switch to troublemaker and spinner of tales had thrown him for a loop.

How on earth was he supposed to respond to her crazy scheme?

It would be better, easier, to make her tell her mother the truth, yet there was a part of him that absolutely understood where she was coming from.

His parents weren't the type to pry, but he was always aware of their gentle probing whenever they called.

Dad would ask about the progress of the house and whether he'd been to visit any of the cousins who lived on the other side of the island. Invariably he'd ask if Zach had seen Kiah or spent time with him, reminiscing a bit about how he and Kiah's father had been both second cousins and the best of friends. And always there was the undercurrent of wanting to know Zach hadn't locked himself away from the world, but was enjoying his time in St. Eustace.

Mum would ask about work, and they'd talk about things like his newly discovered love of gardening, but all the while he was hearing the subtle subtext of concern. The worry she felt, knowing how hurt he'd been by the events that led him to abandon his life in London and move to the Caribbean.

He was honest enough to admit that when speaking to his parents he'd donned a facade of cheerfulness and talked as though life was busy and fun, when it was anything but. When in reality he'd withdrawn into a solitary existence. One that gave him far too much time to brood.

Was that very different from what Gen Broussard had done, when she'd tried to placate her mother?

Slowing to a jog, he approached the path he usually took away from the beach and through a wildlife area, which would extend his run for a few more miles over diverse terrain. At the spot where the sand ended, he stopped and carefully considered what she'd said.

She claimed it wasn't the effects of the Bell's palsy holding her back from having a relationship, and he hoped that was true. Yes, the physical effects were noticeable, as soon as one saw her for the first time, but did little, if anything, to lessen her attractiveness.

At least, as far as he was concerned.

While this was the first time he'd been exposed to her quirkier side, he'd been very aware of her beauty and the energetic charisma that made her a favorite among the hospital staff. Although it really was none of his business, he couldn't help wondering why she was still single. Not that being single and wanting to remain that way was a bad thing. Just that she seemed the type who would have men buzzing about like bees and would bring a great deal of happiness into a man's life.

Which made her mother's worries, and Gen's desire to assuage them, understandable.

Besides, he couldn't help being amused, not only by her way of dealing with her mother, but also by the nerve it must have taken to approach him with her crazy plan. Doing so spoke to an adventurous spirit, which was something he once upon a time would have claimed to share. The younger Zachary had been spontaneous and fun loving, until Moira had told him his "antics," as she called them, were embarrassing.

Now he envied Genevieve her audacity and wished he'd retained some of his own.

But maybe he had, since he found himself wondering what it would hurt to hear her out and perhaps even help? If nothing else, it would get him out of his self-imposed shell and add a bit of sparkle to his life.

There was, after all, no need to feel this deep trepidation. He'd seen combat and lived to tell the tale. Pretending to be involved with a beautiful woman should be a walk in the park.

And it wasn't as though she were really interested in him, as a man or potential partner. She was a surgeon, and he'd already learned the hard way not to do what his father called "flying above his nest." If and when she settled down, he had no doubt it would be with someone far more talented and ambitious than him—another doctor, or a lawyer perhaps.

Not an ex-soldier and RN, who was completely content with his lot.

And since the scheme was hers, and they'd be keeping it totally platonic, it wouldn't affect their work life either.

A truncated bark of laughter forced its way past his throat, and Zach shook his head as he turned and started jogging back. Genevieve Broussard might just be the catalyst he needed to get his life out of the doldrums, and he realized he'd already made the decision.

If she was still at the gazebo and hadn't chosen to abandon her crazy plan, he'd hear her out and, more likely than not, agree to help.

Somehow, he wasn't at all surprised to round the headland and see her in the distance, right where he'd left her but facing the other way so she could see him coming. And when he got closer, he noticed the jelly coconuts on the table, the tops already lopped off, hers with a paper straw in it.

"I got you some coconut water," she said, giving him another of those impish smiles. "Still in the original container."

"Thanks."

He knew he sounded grumpy but didn't do anything to mitigate it. In the back of his mind he still thought she was barking mad to have come up with the scheme, and he was just as crazy to be considering going along with it.

Sitting across from her—and even though it felt as if he was making a colossal mistake— as he unwrapped his straw he looked at her and said, "So, how do you want to proceed?"

And her grin of delight once more almost knocked him off his seat.

CHAPTER THREE

Gᴇɴ ᴄʜᴇᴄᴋᴇᴅ ʜᴇʀ GPS again, as the road she was driving along narrowed to the point where she wondered if another vehicle could pass going in the opposite direction. Zach had warned her he lived out in the "country," although it was only about fifteen minutes away from the hospital. Before they'd left the beach the day before, he'd made her program his address into her phone and checked to make sure the directions were accurate.

"Sometimes, once you get outside of the city, the smaller roads don't appear," he'd said, looking at her phone. "But this looks right."

Now, as she was directed to take the next right, she couldn't help wondering whether the darn app was actually working properly. As far as she could see, the right-hand side of the road was cliff face without even a track in sight.

Just as she was about to find a spot to squeeze over into and call him, she rounded a corner and saw an even narrower road branching off from the main.

"This cycle track he lives on better not scratch my car," she groused aloud, perhaps in an attempt to quell the nervous flutters in her belly.

She still couldn't believe he'd agreed to her harebrained idea. But somehow, and she wasn't at all sure why, he'd given in and invited her up to his place the following evening for supper. She wasn't even sure what he meant by supper since, to her, any meal after six in the evening would be dinner.

Was supper just another way to say dinner, or a completely different type of meal?

Would she have to stop and get a burger on her way home, after being given crackers and cheese or something similar?

Realizing she was thinking like that so as not to dwell too much on the craziness of what she was doing, she chuckled to herself. It didn't matter, really, what he fed her, although she was quite hungry. The important thing was to firm up their plans.

But she knew he had some deep reservations.

"How on earth are we going to fool your mother into believing we've had a months-long relationship, when we don't even really know each other?" he'd asked the day before at the beach.

She'd already given that some thought.

"We each write a list of things a partner would know about us after about five months. A dossier, if you like. That way we can at least talk about stuff together when she's around and make it sound good."

He'd looked extremely skeptical. "What kinds of things?"

"Whatever you think necessary," she'd replied, because she didn't know *exactly* what to tell him. "Pertinent information."

Since he'd worked the morning shift, he probably hadn't even gotten to it, while she'd labored over putting her list together, the chore taking up most of the day.

It had been surprisingly difficult. People thought she was gregarious and outgoing, and she was, to a point. Beyond the superficial, though, she liked to play her cards close to her chest. Figuring out just how much information was enough had been hard. There were things she wouldn't share with anyone right now, much less a stranger she was roping into what amounted to a performance.

She was traveling uphill, along a road that was surprisingly smooth, although it seemed no wider than a deer track through the woods. The wild vegetation that had bordered the main road gave way to banana trees on one side and some sort of citrus grove on the other. In the distance, and farther up the road, she caught a glimpse of a roofline behind the hill, but couldn't see the house although, according to the GPS, she was within mere yards of it.

Then, as she rounded another corner, she came upon a pair of gateposts and, as she turned in, got her first view of the house.

Instinctively easing off the gas, she took in the lovely, if slightly dilapidated, sight, set at the top of a hill above her position.

The base was of irregularly cut stones, stacked perfectly, above which rose the second story's wooden walls, topped with a steep pitched roof decorated with gingerbread trim. To make it even more perfect, there was a wrap-around veranda outside the second story with a colonnade below.

"Whoa," she breathed, absolutely enchanted. She'd always had a soft spot for older, characterful houses, and this one was adorable.

Making her way slowly up the curved driveway, she could see where the bushes alongside had been trimmed back and were bright with yellow flowers. Other parts of the terraced garden seemed rather wild, but there were spots where grass had been cut away, revealing freestanding trees and bushes.

While there was a gravel parking area on one

side, Zach had told her to drive around to the back, and Gen admired the rest of the house as she did. The land at the back was flatter and had what looked like a well-tended vegetable garden, along with a small gazebo under which was a table and four chairs.

Pulling in beside Zach's SUV, she took a moment to admire the house once more while she put the car in Park. Just as she was wondering whether to text him or toot her horn to let him know she was there, the back door opened, and Zach stepped out onto the stoop.

For a moment, she froze, as though seeing him for the first time. Wearing cargo shorts and a T-shirt, he was barefoot and casually yummy. The thought that she'd chosen well, if she wanted to impress and reassure her mother, made her grin, and she saw his lips quirk upward in return.

Grabbing her tote from the seat beside her, she got out, just as he walked down the path toward her car.

"What a glorious house," she said before closing her car door. "Is it yours? How did you find it?"

His smile got a little wider, and Gen realized she'd never heard this man laugh. Not once in five, almost six, months. And suddenly, she wanted to be the one to make that happen.

"It was my grandfather's family home," he replied, meeting her at the end of the path and turning back to gaze up at the house with her. "The family farmed here for generations, but my father and his siblings left the island to live abroad, so there was no one here to take over when Grandad died."

"That's a shame," she said. "But at least the house is still in the family."

"Yeah." He put his hand lightly on the small of her back, saying, "Come on in. Grandad left the property to all his children—four in total—but only my father was thinking of coming back here after he retires, so they split the fifty or so acres up. Dad took the house and five acres, while the rest was doled out between his siblings."

"And you're fixing it up?" she asked, sure she'd heard Kiah say something to that effect the day before at the hospital.

"It definitely needs some work," he replied as she went through the double doors and into a hallway. "Parts of the veranda upstairs weren't safe, and I had some windows replaced, as well as started on painting the outside. I'm trying to work up the stamina to redo the kitchen."

He'd slipped past her and started up a wooden staircase on the left side of the corridor, making her wonder where he was going.

"What's up here?" she asked, even as she had one foot already on the first tread.

He glanced back at her. "It's an upside-down house. All the bedrooms are on the ground floor, where, because of the thick stone walls, it's cooler, and the living spaces are upstairs."

"An upside-down house? I've never heard that expression before. Is that what they call it in England?" Halfway up the steps, she caught the scent of something delicious cooking, which allayed her fears of being starved.

He threw her an amused look over his shoulder. "I thought that was what it was called everywhere."

That made her chuckle, but her laughter died when she got to the top of the staircase and found herself in a huge, square kitchen with doors on both sides, opening onto the veranda and…

"What an amazing view!"

As though drawn by the spell of the verdant land and distant ocean, she moved toward the doors. From its position at the top of the hill, there was a clear view through a valley, which opened up to the sea.

"They really knew how to build back in the day. Excuse me," he added, coming up behind her and then slipping past to go to a cupboard. He left behind a warm, masculine scent that somehow went straight to her head. "The house not only catches the prevailing winds but also has stellar views of sunrise and sunset."

Gen tore herself away from the sight of the sun dipping toward the horizon and, instead, walked over to the table, setting her bag down on one of the chairs.

She wasn't here to drool over the house, the view or Zachary Lewin. She was on a mission.

Pulling out her dossier, she pulled out a chair and sat down.

"I know you probably haven't had a chance to put anything together yet, since you worked today, but here's my information."

"Mine is there," he replied, pointing to a sheaf of papers on the table next to her.

"Oh." Surprised, she picked up the pages and started reading.

"You were in the army?" That certainly explained that straight-backed, solid posture and his level of fitness.

"Yes, for almost ten years."

"What was your rank?"

"Captain."

She giggled. "That'll impress Mom."

He made a noncommittal sound, but when she glanced up at him, he had his back to her, leaving her with no clue what it meant. So, she went back to the list:

He'd thought of almost everything, even things she'd missed, like favorite TV shows and book genres.

"*Doctor Who* fan, huh?"

He was at the stove now, stirring something, and she saw the wide shoulders shrug.

"It's one of the few shows that have stood the test of time. Have you watched it?"

"Some," she admitted absently, still reading. "But not the entire thing."

"Great binge-watching show, if you ever have a year or so to spare."

His dry comment made her snort. "Yeah, right. I count myself lucky when I get two full days off in a row. Or I did, before I came here."

"You worked as a trauma surgeon only, back home?"

"Yes, and unfortunately was kept far busier than I liked." Working in a large central hospital had meant they got more than their fair share of trauma victims, and she'd gotten way too close to burnout. The night she'd found herself sobbing uncontrollably in the ladies' room, having been unable to save the life of a young victim of a drive-by shooting, she'd known it was time for a change.

"How do you find it here?" There was nothing but genuine curiosity in his voice. "It must be a lot different from what you're used to."

"I like it, a lot," she said. Then she had to admit, "At first, I wasn't sure how it would work out. I wasn't used to what felt like a far more leisurely work schedule and had to get back into doing more general and elective surgeries. But after a while, I realized I'd been running on adrenaline for years, and it had taken its toll."

He'd turned to face her while she was talking, leaning casually against the counter, and he nodded.

"It takes a while to get out of flight-or-fight mode, once you've been in it for a while. After I came back from a war zone, it would take me months to come down off high alert."

"Yes," she said, not sure why she was willing—no, eager—to tell him what she'd experienced. "It took me ages to actually sleep straight through the night, without startling awake, sure my phone was ringing and I was being called to the hospital."

He didn't reply but nodded gently, his expression one of complete understanding, and Gen had to look away, back to the papers in front of her, almost in tears.

"Anyway," she said hurriedly, "What else do we have here?"

Zach cleared his throat, the sound unusual enough to have her looking back up at him. He was wearing a rueful smile, but all hints of compassion were gone.

"It's a little late to ask if you like fish, since that's what I cooked. If you don't, I'll take you out somewhere to eat."

She laughed, relieved to have gotten past the awkward moment without making a fool of herself.

"I'm from New Orleans," she reassured him. "If I didn't like seafood, I'd be disowned."

Still no laugh from him, but she did get something close to a grin.

"It's just some steamed fish with okra, onion and carrot, served with brown rice."

"Perfect. And can we eat out on the veranda, so I can watch the sunset?"

Now there was a full-on grin, and it transformed his face from handsome to stunning, making Gen's heart do a funny little flip.

"I already set the table out there," he replied, before turning back to the stove. "It's my favorite place to eat in the evenings."

Suddenly uninterested in what he'd written about himself and more intent on food and more natural conversation, she got up and tapped the pages in her hand into a neat pile.

"Come on then," she said, putting the paper on the table. "What can I carry out for you?"

"If you could grab those trivets, I'll bring

out the food," he said, pointing to a couple of wooden hot pads on the counter.

Doing as he bid, she asked, "So, you're related to Kiah Langdon? How? And do you have any more family still here?"

As they went out onto the veranda and sat down to the delicious meal, she was aware of being—perhaps for the first time in a long time—fully engaged. Interested and relaxed in a way unusual for the life she'd been living.

And the little pang of melancholy she experienced, as she realized it was all too temporary, had to be forced aside.

CHAPTER FOUR

ON THE DAY after his supper with Gen Broussard, Zach woke up just before sunrise, as was his habit. With his cup of tea in hand, he went downstairs and out into the back garden, taking a deep breath of the morning air.

He'd hardly slept the night before, having spent much of the wee hours poring over Gen's biographical information and trying to sort out in his own mind just who *exactly* Genevieve Broussard was.

Having worked with her for months, he'd thought he had some kind of handle on her personality, but the more time he spent with her outside of the hospital the more he realized he had no clue. Turning to her own words—to the things she considered important for him to know—was another effort to figure her out.

The dossier was factual, with one or two surprises, like the information she'd been a contestant in a number of beauty pageants and her talent had been dancing.

But as interesting as her listed information was, the hours they'd spent together the evening before were even more illuminating.

Her avid curiosity, coupled with a mind that flitted unerringly from subject to subject with the precision of a hummingbird, left him slightly shell-shocked trying to keep up. But despite the mental gymnastics she'd put him through, Zach realized it was the best night he'd had in a long, long time.

Yet, after she'd left to go home, Zach realized that while he'd thought she'd been gregarious and outgoing, he'd actually learned very little about her personally.

She'd ferreted a whack more information out of him than she'd revealed about herself by asking him myriad questions and jumping to another topic before he could ask her anything in turn.

It made him wonder what she had to hide, and unfortunately, her dossier didn't offer any answers on that point.

Taking a sip of his tea and admiring the way the treetops were starting to glow with clear golden light, he came to the conclusion that Gen was a master at deflection. If they were to present themselves as a couple, as she wanted, he was going to have to pin her down over certain things. It was all well and good to know where she went to school, that she graduated summa cum laude and where she did her residency, but there was no intimacy to the knowledge.

Zach sighed. So many questions brought up by her sparkling, yet rather mysterious persona.

But he was out of practice in getting women to open up. Out of practice in being a working part of a relationship. Since Moira dumped him, he'd had ample time to reflect on the last few years they'd been together, and all the signs of deterioration had been there. Unfortunately, he'd missed or ignored them and, in some cases, just accepted her assurance that everything was fine when, in reality, it was going down the drain.

The truth was she'd already had one foot out the door and was just making sure she was set career-wise before leaving.

"We've grown apart," she'd said. "It's not the same anymore."

"I've been away for most of the time and have hardly had a chance to settle back into civilian life." Gobsmacked by the sudden turn of events, it was all he could think of to say. Surely Moira would realize this new phase of their relationship needed a chance to work out? With him no longer in the army, her finally being certified as a barrister and them actually living together full-time, everything had changed. "We can make it work. Things are finally more settled—"

"You just don't get it, do you?" The veneer of sadness and regret she'd worn fell away, revealing the cold, hard surface beneath. "I've outgrown you. You'll never be in my league, and I won't be embarrassed by you anymore. I'm moving up in the world, and you'll always be just a boy from Brixton, without ambition or drive."

It was only later, after it was all over, that he'd realized how she'd used him, and how many of his so-called friends knew.

The familiar weight of shame and anger settled on his shoulders, but this time Zach refused to give in to the impulse pushing him toward melancholy. Instead, he took another deep breath and walked over to the gazebo to put his cup on the table. Then he made his way across to his vegetable patch.

Since coming to the island, he'd discovered an interest in and a knack for gardening, aided by Mr. Alexander—or Mass Alex, as he was called—the elderly gentleman who lived down the road. Mass Alex, now in his eighties, had looked after the garden before and after Grandad had died, cutting back as much of the bush as he could manage. Under his tutelage, Zach had started bringing the landscaping back to life and was growing a lot of his own veg.

The tranquility of the land first thing in the morning was one of his favorite things, and as he walked through the neat rows, bending occasionally to pull a weed, he let that peace flow over him.

Yet, his brain wouldn't stop ticking over, thinking about Gen.

Then he realized he was smiling, thinking about her and the crazy scheme he'd signed up for. It was an adventure. A little fun in the midst of a life he'd allowed to grow a bit stale and flat.

Why not just enjoy it?

They'd agreed to meet for lunch so as to be seen together outside of the hospital, setting the stage for the performance to come.

And if Genevieve wanted a boyfriend, that was what Zach would give her.

Hopefully she was fully prepared.

It was only after he'd unhooked the hose from the side of the concrete water tank that he realized he was whistling, and that made him chuckle out loud.

Watch out, Dr. Broussard. Here comes your English lover-man.

Gen slept in, sleepily rolling out of bed just after eight thirty, glad to have the chance for a lazy morning. By nature she wasn't a morning person, and years of having to get up early hadn't changed that, just made her adapt to whatever schedule she was on. So, it was nice to sleep in for a change.

As she sat on the edge of the mattress, her first thought was of Zach Lewin and the evening they'd spent together.

He was a dream, if imaginary, boyfriend, and she couldn't help patting herself on the back for having chosen him—and having gotten him to agree to the farce.

There was no doubt in her mind that her mother would be impressed with Zach. He was nice, respectful and—despite being so good-looking—somehow perfectly ordinary, in an extraordinary way. It had been lovely to simply sit and talk, without worrying about whether he'd try to take advantage of the situation or was somehow judging her.

She was honest enough to admit her past dating life hadn't been as relaxing and fun as last night. With most men she'd been hyperaware of each of her quirks, constantly reminding herself not to talk too much or ask too many questions, but with Zach she could just be herself.

It was a nice change to realize he didn't seem to mind the way she jumped from subject to subject.

He definitely wasn't like the men Gen had dated in the past, but that was probably all for the good. Mom hadn't been terribly impressed with any of them anyway, especially Gen's ex-fiancé.

"Johan was too smooth," she'd said, when she heard about the breakup. "I'd go so far as to say smarmy, considering how things have turned out."

Gen had wanted to argue but couldn't in good conscience disagree. In hindsight she'd realized Johan was more enthralled with the idea of being able to tell people his fiancée was a beauty queen than he'd been enamored with her. Not even her credentials as a surgeon were as important to him as being seen with what he considered a beautiful woman on his arm.

As soon as it became clear the nerve damage was permanent, he'd dropped her faster than a red-hot coal, as though her looks were all she had to recommend her.

Then turned around and married her supposed best friend and fellow pageant contestant.

The hurt had taken her to a dark, dark place. One she'd fought hard to escape. At heart, she was an optimist, and she'd taken to counting her blessings as a way to remind herself how much she had going for her.

A family who had rallied to her side.

A job she loved and believed in and had been able to continue, even after the Bell's palsy.

This new, quieter and more relaxing life on St. Eustace.

Yet, she'd been screwed so tight by everything that had happened and the effort to push it all to the deep recesses of her mind that the stress had almost cost her everything anyway.

Funny to realize that thinking about it now didn't bring the same deep emotional response as usual. Maybe she was actually getting over it all?

Smiling, she hopped out of bed to put on the coffee maker before heading into the bathroom to shower. Just as she'd finished getting dressed and was pouring her first, much needed coffee of the day, her phone rang, causing her to scamper back into the bedroom to find it.

The hospital.

"Hello, Dr. Broussard," said the voice on the other end after Gen had identified herself. "Sorry to bother you, but Director Hamilton asked me to call. We have a patient coming off the cruise ship that's in port, and the ship's doctor suspects a ruptured appendix with possible complications. Dr. Langdon is on the other side of the island, and Dr. Goulding is performing back surgery. Can you come in?"

"Of course," Gen said, pushing aside a spurt

of annoyance and regret. She was supposed to meet up with Zach for lunch and, depending on how bad the patient was, she might not be able to make it. "I'll be there in about fifteen minutes."

Ruefully, she poured her highly anticipated coffee into a travel mug, then found Zach's number as she headed into the bedroom to change into scrubs. Might as well be prepared, rather than have to change again when she got to the hospital.

"Hey there," she said when he picked up. "I might have to cancel lunch. I've been called in to the hospital."

"I have too," he replied, and she heard a car door slam. "One of the surgical nurses called in sick."

"Oh." Knowing they might be operating together shouldn't bring that little tingle of pleasure. "Well then, I'll see you there."

"Yes," he said, and for some reason it sounded as though he were smiling too. "See you in a few."

Her townhouse wasn't very far from the hospital, so she was there within the time range she'd specified.

As she was heading down the hallway from the staff entrance, she saw Director Hamilton farther along and stopped when he said, "I'm sorry to call you in on your day off, Genevieve, but you're the most experienced surgeon we have available right now."

"No problem." She gave him a smile, knowing that with Kiah and John unavailable, it was either her or one of the younger doctors who'd have to operate. And coming from an area where tourism was important too, Gen knew the director would be nervous about having one of the visitors to the island operated on in their hospital. "I don't mind."

"Thank you. I appreciate it very much. The patient is on her way by ambulance from the port and should be here within minutes."

As the director patted her shoulder, Gen heard the outside door open behind her and footsteps approaching. Even without turning, she knew it was Zach, but glanced back anyway.

He was smiling, and something about that grin had her brain scrambling and goose bumps rushing across her torso and arms.

"Morning, Director," he said when he was still a couple of paces away. Then he turned his dark, somehow mischievous gaze on Gen, and she froze.

"Morning, Zach..."

The director's words trailed away as Zach paused and, bending his head, kissed Gen on her cheek, leaving a warm, electrically charged spot on her skin.

"Morning, love," he murmured, and Gen swore she heard barely suppressed laughter in his deep, soft tone. "Sleep well?"

"Y...yes, thank you," was all she could get out past the lump of mingled horror and laughter clogging her throat. "You?"

"Never better," he replied.

Then he strolled away as casual as could be, leaving Gen biting the inside of her cheek, hardly daring to look at Director Hamilton. When she finally risked a glance, the other man, thankfully, was gaping at Zach's retreating figure.

By the time the director turned his startled gaze her way, Gen had some semblance of control over herself, and she gave him one of her best smiles.

"Well, I better get ready for when the patient arrives. See you later, Director."

Quick walking for all she was worth, she almost caught up to Zach near the staff changing rooms, but he swerved into the nurses' lounge, leaving her high and dry in the walkway.

"What the hell?" she muttered to the now empty corridor. She still couldn't make up her mind whether to laugh or be angry. Neither seemed exactly appropriate, but what else *to* feel? "What the coo-calloo-calloo?"

Then she heard the wail of the approaching ambulance and shook her head, pushing all of it aside, as she hurried toward emerge.

She'd deal with Zachary Lewin later.

Oh, yes. She would.

CHAPTER FIVE

MRS. BATTEN, THE patient from the cruise ship, was in extreme pain and already running a high fever by the time she arrived at the hospital. After taking a history and examining the patient, Gen agreed with the cruise ship doctor's prognosis. Further tests pointed not just to a ruptured appendix, but also peritonitis.

"It's my first cruise, and I didn't want to miss it," Mrs. Batten said in between groans.

She admitted to having pain before she boarded the ship, but convinced herself that it was nothing more than nerves and excitement. As the severity increased, she'd finally sought medical attention on board.

"Unfortunately, you're going to miss the rest of the cruise," Gen told her gently. "I'm going to operate to remove the appendix and clean up any infected tissue, but you'll be here in the hospital for at least a few days."

"I don't even care anymore," her patient said, her eyes closed. "I just want the pain to go away."

It was up to Gen to explain to the woman's worried husband just how serious his wife's situation was.

"I'll have a better idea of how severe her condition is when I operate, but she may have to be in hospital for a while," she told Mr. Batten.

"Do whatever you need to," the man said, his eyes misty, although he was making a valiant effort to hold himself together. "Just make her well, please. We were celebrating our third wedding anniversary, and I really want to make it to thirty at least with her."

Entering the presurgery meeting with the team, Gen gave Zach a sour look and then put him and his foolishness aside, running down her findings and her expectations.

"From her T cell count and the scans, I suspect this will be a long one, folks."

Her pronouncement was greeted with a murmur, and then it was all hands on deck.

The operating room was already set up, and Gen went to scrub in while the patient was transported from emergency.

As it turned out, she'd been right in her assessment. Removing the ruptured appendix and all infected tissue was a long, painstaking job, and it was almost one in the afternoon before Gen was able to close.

Once Mrs. Batten was in the recovery room, the surgical team handed over to the ICU staff, and Gen, Zach and the other surgical nurse, Monica, started walking back toward the desk.

Gen decided, with Monica as witness, this was as good a time as any to get back at Zach for his earlier mischief.

"Hey," she said in the most casual tone ever. "Are we still on for lunch? I'm starved."

From the corner of her eye, she saw Monica do a double take and had to bite her lip not to giggle.

But Zach didn't sound at all fazed as he replied, "Sure. Do you mind swinging by the house first, though? I left in such a hurry I didn't pack a change of clothes."

"I didn't either," she answered, making her voice light and airy. "How about we meet somewhere? I have to go and update Mr. Batten, and then I can leave."

"How about Nectar on the Beach?" he asked. By now, Monica wasn't even pretending not to listen but was avidly soaking in the entire conversation.

"Perfect." She gave him a dazzling, beauty queen smile, suddenly wishing it were as bright and symmetrical as it used to be. "Meet you there in about forty minutes?"

And, as soon as he agreed, she strode off, chuckling to herself.

He was surely in for a grilling from the rest of the nursing staff, and it served him darn well right.

She wasted no time taking him to task too, when they met up at the seaside restaurant, getting right on his case as soon as she sat across from him at the table overlooking the rolling surf.

"What got into you this morning?" she demanded, giving him a glare, although she really wanted to laugh.

Maybe he saw the amusement in her eyes, because his lips twitched upward slightly before he said, "Hey, just setting the scene."

"But in front of the director? Really?"

Zach shrugged. "I saw him there and realized that if it gets back to him that we're dating, he might worry about our ability to work together. The operation today was already scheduled, and we both know what we're doing won't make a difference to our jobs, so it was a good way to get ahead of any concerns he might have."

Gen thought it through for a moment and then couldn't help the smile forcing its way onto her mouth.

"Okay, I have to admit that's genius."

He smiled back, but the rest of the conversation was put on hold by the waiter coming to take their drink order and give them menus. Once they'd chosen their meals and ordered, the conversation became more general, as they discussed the various restaurants they'd visited since coming to the island.

Only after they'd eaten some of their meal did Gen jump to a subject she found interesting and wanted to know more about.

"How did you end up in the army?"

Zach didn't look up right away, but she saw his eyebrows twitch upward for an instant.

His voice was calm and factual, though, as he replied, "My parents wanted me to go to uni after I finished comprehensive, and I started but realized it wasn't for me."

"What do you mean?"

He met her gaze then, and she was at a loss as to what it was she was seeing in his expression.

"Well, firstly, I was tired of sitting in classrooms all the time, although I didn't mind the studying. Secondly, I realized how much it was going to end up costing for me to stay in uni and opted for military training instead."

"What did your parents think about that?" she asked before taking a bite of her delicious fish taco.

"Mum was fine with it, but Dad was a bit disappointed. He was banking on me being the first in the family to graduate from university. I did point out to them that I still planned to get a degree, just not in the way they expected. Besides, my younger sister is the true brains in the family, so it was better they concentrate on her going on to higher education."

"Did she get a degree?"

He smiled slightly. "Two, actually."

"Did you ever consider becoming a doctor instead of a nurse?"

Now the glance he threw her was truly unfathomable, but it made the back of her neck prickle for some reason.

"Didn't really want to spend the time necessary," he replied in the kind of laconic tone people use when they don't want to continue the conversation.

"I think you'd have been excellent at it," she said honestly. "But having gone through the slog myself, I can completely understand."

"I'm happy with what I've achieved," he said in an even more quelling voice, which only served to pique her curiosity and make her want to dig deeper.

"Oh, but—"

He held up his hand, stopping her midsentence. "No. My turn to ask some questions. How did you get into pageants?"

A little taken aback at the quick change of subject, which was usually her modus operandi, Gen shrugged.

"I was one of those kids who couldn't keep still, so my parents put me in dance class. One of the other students' mother was into pageant organization and talked my mother into letting me enter one to see how I'd like it, and I just kept doing it."

In reality, she'd kept doing it because it had given her a chance to spend more time with Loren, whose mother had gotten her involved, and she would have sworn her friend felt the same way. It was only years later she realized that in Loren's mind they'd been competing, not just for titles and crowns but for Loren's mother's attention.

And eventually, for men.

Hopefully Loren was content with the big win, and Johan was making her happy, although Gen knew that sometimes what you consider a prize turns out to be not one at all.

She pushed the unhappy thoughts aside as Zach asked, "Did you keep on because you enjoyed it, or was there some other reason?"

She considered how to answer, unwilling

to bring up Loren, as she ate the last bite of her meal.

"I did enjoy it," she finally said. "I was mostly involved in charity pageants, and that was satisfying in itself. And I know people think there're all fluff, with the contestants wanting to cat fight all the time, but it isn't really like that at all. It can be quite empowering, if you go into it with the right attitude. Besides, I got to see places I probably wouldn't otherwise, and build some really solid relationships with other women." Sending him a teasing smile, she added, "And I got to wear clothing I never would have in any other setting."

His lips quirked at that, although she got the feeling he saw through her attempt at humor. Talking about that time of her life was still both pleasure and pain, although now she could look back at it with a bit more equanimity.

"So, why did you give it up?"

Startled, she gave him a long, searching look, before answering, "I stopped when I was doing my residency because that was, of course, most important. Then, when I was considering doing one more..."

She touched the corner of her mouth. The immobile part that had effectively scotched any hopes she might have had of winning one of the major pageants.

He didn't reply at once but lifted his hand to get the waiter's attention. When the man came over, Zach said, "Do you have the bread pudding on the menu today?"

"Yes, sir," the waiter replied with a grin. "Can I get you one?"

"Two," came the immediate reply.

"Right away, sir."

"Bread pudding?" Gen questioned with eyebrows raised.

"You won't regret it," he said. "I promise. They make it with dark chocolate and a rum sauce that's absolutely splendid."

She gave a little giggle. "I get such a kick out of some of the things you say. 'Absolutely splendid' is up there with my favorites."

"You're a fine one to talk. What was that I heard you say today in theater when you realized just how badly infected Mrs. Batten was?"

Warmth spread up into her cheeks. "Yeah, it's a cussword I made up long ago, and sometimes it slips out."

Was that a chuckle issuing from Zach's throat? It was so brief Gen couldn't even be sure, and before she could say anything more the waiter was back with their dessert.

"Oh, my, goodness." She stared at the confection on her plate and inhaled the glorious scent rising up to tease her nostrils.

"I told you," he said, reaching for his fork. But then he paused with it hovering over the plate and said, "I think you should have entered that last pageant if you'd really wanted to."

Startled, she shook her head. "Not after the Bell's, I couldn't."

His brow creased, and his eyes narrowed slightly. "You're still beautiful. And a well-respected surgeon. Think of all the little girls you'd have inspired if you'd put yourself out there again."

The wave of surprised pleasure his words gave her made heat rise up her chest and into her face, and she wanted to look away, but the intensity of his gaze kept hers snared.

For a long moment she forgot.

Forgot this was just a farce and the handsome man looking at her with such surety from across the table wasn't a love interest. Not even really a friend, although she hoped they were on the way there.

Instead, her body grew warm with pleasure and something far too close to desire to be comfortable, and she had to force her thoughts away from wondering if he really meant it or was just being kind.

But she got herself back under control and gave him what would have been an award-winning smile back in the days when her smile was considered one of her best assets.

"I would never consider doing another pageant," she said truthfully, but with all the amusement she could muster in her voice.

The furrows in his brow deepened. "Why not?"

"Because I'd have to forgo pleasures like this bread pudding, and I'm no longer willing to make those kinds of terrible, if noble, sacrifices."

Zach laughed.

There was no mistaking it.

Not a chuckle, but a full-on laugh, and now the pleasure she felt before was magnified until it filled her to the brim, and she laughed along with him.

Zach watched Gen eat the bread pudding and couldn't help smiling to himself. She treated it as though it were a gift from the gods, each bite to be savored with a little hum of enjoyment.

She even gazed with what looked like longing at her empty plate and scooped the last of the sauce into her mouth with the side of her fork.

"That was...decadent," she sighed, placing the fork back on her plate. "Thank you for ordering it."

"I'm glad you enjoyed it," he replied. "It suddenly occurred to me that I should have asked you if you wanted it." He shrugged ruefully. "I've been told I'm too take-charge at times."

Actually, what he'd been accused of was making arrogant assumptions, which still hurt, since all he'd ever tried to do was make Moira happy with little gestures and gifts he thought she'd like.

He'd been completely wrong about that.

"Well, if I didn't want it, I'd have canceled the order," Gen said in a serene tone. "Believe me, I'd have no problem doing that."

"Good," he said. "Tell me if you think I'm overstepping my bounds."

"Will do."

She was smiling as she said it, making him wonder what she was thinking, but before he could ask she got down to business.

"So, since you've set the scene at the hospital, there are a few things we should discuss if we're going to make this work in front of my mother."

"What kinds of things?"

"Well, like how affectionate we should be toward each other in public," she replied, straightfaced. "Especially around my mom."

For some reason, her words made a tingle run up his spine, but he tried to match her matter-of-fact attitude.

"How will she expect us to act?"

He hadn't even thought about that aspect of things and was genuinely surprised that it didn't make him feel in the slightest bit uncomfortable.

In fact, being honest with himself, he was rather looking forward to seeing how far she expected them to go.

"Well, she knows I'm pretty affectionate by nature," Gen said slowly. "So, she'll expect us to touch each other, although—you know—respectfully, in front of her."

The tingling settled low in his back, and he had to resist the urge to shift in his seat.

Clearly there needed to be some other, clear-cut rules put in place.

Not for Gen, who seemed completely sanguine about the entire thing. But he was suddenly having to push aside some pretty risqué imaginings.

"It'll be like performing a play, yeah? We're just playing the parts your mum expects us to, so we have to learn our lines and coordinate our actions to make it believable."

Gen's face lit up with one of her beaming, beguiling smiles.

"Yes!" she exclaimed, as though he'd made a profound pronouncement. "That's it exactly. And we'll have a bit of time to practice, so it'll be perfect."

Somehow that did nothing to dispel the idea

forming at the back of his mind that he was in beyond his depth.

But all he said in reply was, "All the world's a stage, and all the men and women merely players."

"And he knows Shakespeare too." Gen beamed at him across the table. "Mom's gonna *love* you!"

CHAPTER SIX

FROM HIS TONE when she suggested it, Gen wasn't sure Zach was too enthused by the thought of them practicing to behave like a couple in love. Yet, after a few days, he seemed to be totally into the role.

He was completely professional at work, but when they met up afterward, as they did almost every evening, anyone seeing them together would absolutely believe they were a couple.

Holding her hand or putting his palm on the small of her back to guide her up the stairs.

Whispering into her ear, even though what he was saying was usually something prosaic, and totally un-lover-like.

Smiling at her, as though she were everything and a bucket of chicken.

He even took her out to a club one Friday night, and danced with her to a couple of smoochy slow songs.

Gen reminded herself it was all make-believe,

but had to admit that being held tenderly in Zach's arms was the sort of memory a woman could cling to forever.

His muscular body against hers had been thrilling and had made her feel feminine in a way she couldn't recall feeling before.

Not even when dressed in eveningwear with a tiara on her head.

All in all, besides the feeling that perhaps she'd bitten off more than she could chew, she was pleased with the progress of their deception.

The only person who took her to task about it was Mina, and even though she did it in a pretty gentle way, Gen was still left feeling a bit like a worm.

"Zach Lewin?" Mina asked her, having cornered her in the doctor's lounge where, thankfully, it was just the two of them at the time. "Gen, what are you thinking? And how on earth did you rope him into your crazy plan?" Then her face got stern. "It is part of your crazy plan, isn't it? You aren't just leading him on to get your mom off your back, are you?"

"What? No." Gen was quick to tell her, feeling unaccountably hurt that Mina would think her capable of that kind of underhanded behavior. "I explained what I'd done to him, and he agreed to help me out. He's a great guy."

"He is," Mina said, still not looking too happy about the whole affair. "And that's why I'm worried."

"What are you talking about?" It sounded as if there was a story there, and Gen's curiosity was piqued.

"Just that I don't want to see him get into anything that might make life hard for him. He's been through enough."

But when Gen tried to get her to elaborate, Mina was stubbornly silent, only adding, "Don't hurt him."

Gen didn't know why Mina was so worried. As Zach himself had said, they were just playing roles for a little while, and once her mom went back to New Orleans, things would go back to how they'd been before.

"Mom finally called and told me she's coming," she told Zach a week before her mother was due to arrive. "I had to act surprised and delighted."

They were outside in his "veg patch," as he called it, Gen sitting under the gazebo, watching him weed and water and pick some greens to go with their dinner.

He sent her a teasing glance. "You're not delighted that your mother is coming to visit? I thought you liked her."

Looking around for something to toss at him,

she came up empty and had to be satisfied with sticking out her tongue.

"You know what I mean."

Zach just laughed and went back to his gardening.

Strange to think how badly she'd wanted to make him laugh before, and now it was a re-occurring event whenever they were together.

Somehow that warmed her heart in a way she probably shouldn't allow but couldn't seem to control.

A rustling from the bushes nearby had her half out of her chair, until she spotted a pair of yellow, feline eyes staring out at her, and she relaxed again.

"Holy cow, your cat scared me half to death," she told Zach, who straightened from where he'd been uprooting a stalk of scallion. "I didn't know what was going to spring out of the bushes at me."

"There aren't any big predators here in St. Eustace," he said. "So, no need to worry on that score. And, for the record, I don't have a cat."

As he was speaking, the feline in question slunk out of the bushes, giving Gen a side-ways, somehow disapproving look, and headed straight for the man who'd just disavowed it. Once it got up to Zach, it proceeded to twine around his ankles in a rather seductive fashion, pausing to meow plaintively.

"Are you sure about that?" Gen asked, giggling at Zach's baffled expression. "It sure looks like you do."

"I don't even like cats," he said, promptly belying that by bending to scratch behind the cat's ears in what was, apparently, the perfect way.

The ginger beast melted onto its back on the path, gazing up with sloe-eyed adoration when Zach switched to rubbing its belly.

"Well, whether you like them or not seems a moot point to me, right now."

"It must be one of the cats from the farm." Zach straightened, which had the kitty jumping to its feet to resume its previous ankle dance. "But although she doesn't look malnourished, I can feel her bones."

Gen didn't comment on how concerned he seemed over a cat he didn't own, but said, "Well, clearly it needs some fattening up, and it's decided you're the man for the job."

That gained her a shrug, but she wasn't at all surprised when, before they ate, he took a bowl of water and a tin of tuna down to the cat, who'd taken up residence on one of the chairs under the gazebo.

While they were eating, she broached a subject she'd been dreading a bit.

"Did you notice that we only worked together once this week? Do you think that was by design?"

The last thing she wanted was for their "relationship" to affect their work life.

But Zach shook his head. "That's happened before," he pointed out. "And the operation we worked on together was a tricky one. If anyone had any doubts about our ability to work together, they wouldn't have us working on the most intricate surgery of the week."

"True," she said. "I just don't want either of us to be sidelined in any way because of what I've gotten us into."

Zach laughed.

"I worked twelve hours on Wednesday, and I know you slept at the hospital after that little girl's esophageal surgery, so I don't think either of us can complain about being underutilized."

"True," she agreed, relaxing with relief. "I didn't think of it that way."

"What time is your mother coming in?"

The change of subject was welcome, and Gen jumped on it.

"Five o'clock on the twelfth. And she'll be here for ten days. I'm going to try to take some time off to spend with her, but I told her I can't take ten days off from work. I'm lucky if they let me have any at all, since I haven't even been here for a year."

"I've been working at the hospital even less time, so I'm afraid I can't take any vacation days."

Gen waved her hand. "That's fine. Mom can't expect us to be able to drop everything to entertain her while she's here, especially when she decides to 'surprise' me."

Zach smiled. "Luckily for me, my parents are scrupulous planners. They'd never turn up here out of the blue. It took them five years of planning to go to Portugal. Mind you, it took them that long to save up for it too."

Gen nodded, recognizing how privileged her family really was but not willing to say so. "There are studies that say the anticipation of a vacation induces as much pleasure as the vacation itself. Sometimes even more."

He gave her an amused glance. "I'm glad to report that they enjoyed the trip so much that Mum has consistently tried to encourage Dad to retire there instead of here."

"Is your mother from St. Eustace too?"

That was one of the few things he hadn't covered in his dossier.

"No. She was born in Glasgow. Dad met her after he moved to England. Hang on," he added, getting up. "I have a picture of my family I can show you."

He went inside, and she heard him going down the steps to the ground floor. In short order he was back, with a silver-colored frame in hand.

"My mother gave this to me when I was going to university, so it's old," he said, putting it in her hand.

It showed a smiling group, shaded from his dark-skinned father to his very fair mother and their four children, who ranged in every hue in between. She could see Zach got his broad chest and stature from his father, but the shape of his face, nose and eyes came from his mother.

Bending over her shoulder, he pointed out the various members. His breath brushed her cheek, making her entire face tingle. "My dad, mum, Cameron, Catriona and Benjamin."

"And you," she added, smiling at the young, grinning Zach. "Your mother is a redhead," she added. "That explains your freckles, I guess?"

He chuckled, still leaning over her, causing her heart to pound and goose bumps to fan out across her chest and arms. "Actually, although she's a redhead, she doesn't have freckles. Those come from my father's family."

"Funny how that works, isn't it?" she replied,

sounding a little breathless even to herself. "I like your names too."

It was the only thing she could think of to say with his lovely fresh scent filling her head and the heat of his chest warming her nape.

He straightened as she handed him back the photo, leaving her with a sense of loss that was inexplicable.

"We're all named after relatives. Thankfully Mum refused to name me Zachariah, after my grandfather, and got Dad to agree to Zachary. Cameron and Catriona are named after Mum's parents, while Ben is named after Kiah Langdon's father. His father and mine were best friends growing up."

"Wow, so much history," she said, finding some equilibrium now he had retreated to the other side of the table again. "I love that."

"Kiah got the short end of the stick," he said with a chuckle. "He's Hezekiah, named after my father."

And being able to laugh with him dispelled the last vestiges of her tingles, and her heart rate slowed down to a normal pace once more.

Zach leaned back as the deepening shadows cast Gen's face into a mysterious, gorgeous study in gray scale. They were sharing companionable silence, while she watched the final colors of the setting sun fade from the sky, and he found himself equally enthralled by her profile. The more time he spent with her, the more fascinated he found himself becoming.

It was all well and good to say they were play-acting in an effort to fool the people around them, but he knew, for him, the acting was starting to feel far too real.

Leaning over her earlier, he'd realized he was tempted to kiss the top of her head or her cheek.

It had been a long time since he'd felt drawn to another person the way he was to Gen. He could spend hours with her and never feel bored or uncomfortable—except when his body reacted to hers in untoward ways, like when they'd danced together.

Whew.

That had been far too real for comfort.

She'd moved like silk in his arms, her lush body swaying in perfect time with his. It had been easy to imagine they really were a couple, and all he had to do was dip his head and she'd lift hers for a kiss.

Which was something he'd been thinking about way too often.

Kissing Gen.

It had crossed his mind repeatedly that kissing her on her cheek when her mother was around would seem highly unusual. After all, they were supposedly in the midst of a monthslong relationship. Wouldn't it be more natural for them to greet each other with a kiss on the lips?

But that was a direction he was chary of going in, since he wasn't sure he was ready to take such a step.

It seemed far too dangerous to go down that path, especially with his heightened awareness of the attraction building toward the beautiful woman across from him.

What he was beginning to feel for her was way too close to desire to be entirely comfortable, despite the fact it would make his performance all the more realistic.

Shaking the thoughts away, he got up to turn on the lights in the house and catch his breath.

"Would you like some pudding?" he asked, as a way to distract himself. "I have some stewed local plums and ice cream."

The sound of her little chuckle made him smile too.

"That's not pudding. That's fruit and ice cream. But no, thank you." Her chair creaked as he watched her get up. "I'm going to head home. I'm operating early tomorrow morning."

As she spoke, she came into the kitchen, blinking at the brightness of the light. When she rubbed her left eyelid, he realized she was probably more tired than she was letting on.

"Okay," he said, his brain unerringly going back to his previous thoughts about kissing. "Drive carefully, and let me know when you get home."

"Will do," she replied, taking up her handbag. "And why don't you come by my place tomorrow evening for a change. I'm so in love with your house, I keep coming here, making you cook for me. It's time I returned the favor."

He chuckled. "I don't mind. I like cooking."

And he liked having her there. She brought new life to the house, blowing away the cobwebs of his previous funk.

"And I very much like eating your cooking," she agreed serenely, as they walked to the stairs. "But come by anyway. I have a hankering for steak, done on the grill."

"I'd like that," he admitted, and it was no lie. He'd only glimpsed the inside of her townhouse when he'd gone to pick her up for one of their excursions. It would be nice to get a more intimate look. "You need me to bring anything?"

"Nope."

They were at the foot of the steps when she paused, looking up at him, and something in her expression froze him in place.

"Zach," she said softly, coming a little closer. "I'm going to kiss you. If you have any objections, now's the time to voice them."

His throat was suddenly so tight it rendered him unable to voice anything at all. So instead, he opened his arms to her, reminding himself it was all just playacting, even as his body hardened and his heart rate went into overdrive.

She smiled slightly, but it had an uncertain edge to it, and he saw the color staining her cheeks just before she stepped into his arms.

And even though he tried to hold back, he couldn't resist moving his mouth against hers, deepening the kiss in minute increments until he felt the tip of her tongue touch his lower lip.

Then all bets were off.

CHAPTER SEVEN

Gen wasn't sure how she made it home in one piece after the kisses she'd shared with Zach the night before.

All she knew was that by the time they broke apart, her insides felt like jelly, and desire was raging like a wildfire through her veins.

Coo-calloo-calloo, that man could *kiss*.

It had come to her as she sat across from him, listening to him talk about his family and watching his mouth move, that they were going to have to get used to kissing, at least enough to fool her mom. Convincing herself it was one more part of their performance that needed to be rehearsed was easy, but she hadn't been able to figure out how to broach the subject with him. So, in her typical jump-in-with-both-feet style, she decided to just go for it.

Well, she'd gotten a heck of a lot more than she'd planned.

It was seared into her brain—his taste, the

sensation of his body against hers, the heat inundating her, the way she'd plastered herself to him, wanting to get closer and closer.

The latter memory made her bury her head beneath her pillow and groan in distress.

Or was that a moan of desire?

Hard to tell, since her body still thrummed and tingled, reminding her how sexy Zach really was and how much she'd like to find out if he was as skilled a lover as he was a kisser.

Dragging herself out of an exceptionally rumpled bed, she took a cold shower to help her wake up and squelch the need shimmering under her skin.

Luckily, Zach was off that day. She wasn't ready to see him just yet. Later, when he came by for dinner, was soon enough.

Putting the memories aside was easier once she was immersed in the hospital atmosphere, and her scheduled operations went as planned, although she was worried about one patient, who had clotting issues. She ran out after her shift to pick up what she planned to cook that evening, but swung by the hospital one more time to make sure the night shift nurses were fully apprised of the situation before heading home.

It was only after she was driving away from the hospital for the second time that she remembered she hadn't put in for time off. Between operating and the distraction of kissing Zach the night before, it had slipped her mind. It would have to wait until she was back at work in two days. Hopefully the director would be able to accommodate her request.

After quickly showering, she found herself slathering on some of her favorite vanilla-scented lotion. She hadn't used it since coming to St. Eustace, and the realization that she was doing so now because it made her feel lovely and desirable gave her pause.

What on earth was she doing?

Here Zach was, trying to do her a favor, and she was in the process of trying to make it all more complex by beginning to fall for him.

She deserved a kick in the pants!

Putting the bottle back down on the shelf with a snap, she marched out into her bedroom and pulled on a T-shirt and dungaree shorts.

There, she thought, looking at herself in the mirror. There was no less seductive outfit in the world, unless she switched the dungarees for a stretched-out pair of sweats.

And, she told herself sternly while putting the steaks to marinate, there would be no more of that kissing business, unless they had to up their game in front of her mother.

That determination lasted until she opened

her front door and saw Zach standing on the stoop.

"Hey," she said, battling the urge to grab the hunk of scrumptiousness standing there. "Come on in."

He wasn't smiling this evening, and as she led the way toward her covered patio, she wondered if she'd messed everything up with her actions the night before.

But when they got partway through her living room, she felt him touch her arm and paused.

And when he pulled her into his arms, she did nothing at all to resist.

In fact, she was immediately pliant and willing.

Way too willing, she thought hazily as his mouth found hers.

Then she couldn't think anymore.

Just feel.

And want.

"I doubt this is a good idea." His voice was deliciously raspy, and still only a millimeter away from hers. "And I know it wasn't a part of the act, but you taste so delicious, I can't resist."

"Then don't," she replied, before pulling his head back down for another long, drugging kiss.

When they finally pulled apart, she was glad to note she wasn't the only one having a hard time breathing.

"Sorry," he said, although he looked anything but repentant. "But I spent almost all of last night and today wanting to do that."

She rubbed at the corner of her eye, still a bit dazed, wondering if she should admit it had been the same for her, but finally deciding discretion was the better part of valor.

Clearing her throat, she said, "Well, you didn't see me objecting, did you?"

"No," he agreed, still stern-faced. "But it's probably not something we should do much more of. I'll be honest and tell you it could lead to complications neither of us are ready for."

Contemplating his words, she realized what he was trying to oh, so politely say.

He might be tempted to sleep with her, but wasn't interested in a relationship.

That shouldn't hurt, but it did and, in a way she was glad, since it threw a nice bucketful of cold water on her raging lust.

"Understood," she said, finding a smile from somewhere deep inside. "Come on outside so I can fire up the grill. If I don't get it going soon, we'll be eating in the middle of the night."

Then she walked away, glad to have her back to him so he couldn't see her expression.

With some effort, she was able to find the wherewithal to fall back into the easy companionship they'd shared up to that point. In fact, it was easier than she thought it would be, but a lot of that had to do with Zach, who acted as though those kisses had never happened.

"Bagged salad?" he teased, when he wandered into the kitchen as she was putting the rest of the meal together. "You're in the Caribbean, where you can get the freshest veg you could ever want, and you buy a bag of salad?"

She sent him a baleful look. "Hey, not everyone has a veggie garden outside their back door. Besides, for one, this is local produce, just prepackaged." Emphasizing the words with an upheld finger, she added another to make her next point. "And two, because I've been eating at your house so often, I had to toss out a bunch of stuff that had gone off. Don't judge."

He chuckled. "Okay, but next time, just let me bring the veg, yeah?"

The steaks came out perfectly, and for once she timed it just right, so the baked potatoes were done at the same time as the meat.

"This is something I'd never cook at home with my parents," she explained. "We eat a lot more rice and, for some reason, my father dislikes baked potatoes. I didn't learn how to bake a potato until I went to college. Isn't that funny?"

"It really isn't until you leave home that you realize the deficiencies in your real-life education," he agreed. "Mum made sure all of her children knew how to cook and clean, but somehow I missed the lessons on laundry." He chuckled. "Well, to be honest, I was the messiest of all her children and she got tired of waiting for me to do my laundry, so she kept doing it. Probably afraid I'd just wear the dirty clothes."

Gen laughed. "I can't even imagine that. Your place is always immaculate."

"The military very quickly breaks you of those kinds of bad habits."

"Ah, yes. I can see how it would."

They resolutely kept the atmosphere light, the conversation flitting across a bunch of subjects, but Gen couldn't shake the desire shivering in her belly each time she looked at him.

So she was relieved when, as he was leaving, Zach made no move to kiss her again.

Relieved, and severely disappointed.

They'd agreed to go to the beach together the next day as they were both off from work. So the next morning found Gen standing, coffee in hand, looking at the bathing suits she'd laid out on the bed.

Bikini or one-piece?

Taking a sip of her morning wake-up juice, she contemplated her motivations for even giving it this much thought.

She'd always tried to be scrupulously honest with herself and knew she was prone to impulsive, ill-conceived ideas. For all the control she had to exert in her job, she'd never outgrown the habit of doing things outside of work others would consider outlandish. Even outrageous.

Case in point—Zachary Lewin and her roping him into a fake relationship.

One she now was thinking she'd like to make real. Or at the very least, physical.

There was something about him she found infinitely attractive. Not just his looks, although no red-blooded woman would disagree those on their own weren't enough. But he had other, less quantifiable characteristics that she found terribly appealing.

His steadiness, and how easy it was to be with him just hanging out and talking. The way he'd figured out how to rein her in when she'd been inclined to bulldoze through a conversation, doing it in a way she couldn't take offence to or that made her self-conscious.

That intent, focused way he looked at her when she spoke, which told her he was completely there, concentrating on what she was saying. Listening, not planning what he wanted to say when she was through.

And, she'd finally admitted—actually out

loud to herself in the shower—that she wanted him, physically.

Okay, she wasn't really the affair kind of woman. When others in college had been sowing wild oats, Gen had had a couple of long-term relationships. It had never felt comfortable to just sleep with a guy because of a physical urge. Her head, at the very least, had to be engaged too.

Not necessarily her heart though, right?

She knew, without a doubt, Zach wasn't interested in a relationship with her. Although he hadn't come right out and said it, she could read between the lines. So, if she was going to get in any deeper with him, she had to keep that in mind. It did no good to take the pie-in-the-sky approach.

An optimist she might be, but not an idiot.

If she put herself out there, and he didn't take her up on the offer, she'd be the only one embarrassed, right? So why not at least try?

"Bikini it is."

Not the skimpiest of them. That would be too obvious. But she had one in a light blue, batik-inspired print that fit her to a tee and showcased the new and improved curves she'd acquired since giving up pageants.

Curves she'd grown to like a lot and enjoy. In contests they were expected to maintain a slim figure, without any exaggerated physical features, and Gen had been able to keep her size down because she was, at the time, so active. After the Bell's palsy she'd concentrated on maintaining a healthy weight and getting enough exercise to keep strong without overdoing any of it.

Looking into the mirror, she couldn't help giving herself a little smirk. If Zach found her even slightly attractive, and his kisses said he did, this swimsuit should only increase his interest.

"You're a bad, bad girl," she told her reflection, but the smile on her lips said, *I don't care*.

She put on a rather shapeless terry cloth cover-up, just before Zach knocked on the door to pick her up.

"Good morning," she trilled, giving him a wide smile as she closed her front door and locked it. "Perfect day for the beach."

"It is," he said. "Did you bring sunscreen?"

She gave him a sidelong glance as they walked to the car. "I did, and I put some on already. Did you?"

He opened her door for her and had the nerve to smile as he replied, "No, I forgot."

She'd have taken him to task, but he'd already closed her door, and she had the pleasure of watching him walk around the front of the car.

By the time he'd gotten to the driver's side, she was completely distracted and forgot.

The beach wasn't very full, since it was a weekday, so they had their choice of spots to set up the umbrella Zach had brought and spread Gen's beach blanket beneath it. Although it was blazing hot, the sea breeze kept the temperature bearable, and Gen had to admit the sea view was one of the loveliest she'd ever seen. The sky was like a cerulean bowl above their heads, and the water, aquamarine near the dazzling sandy shore and ultramarine where the seabed fell away, was capped by little hits of white froth.

"I'm going in," Zach said after he'd arranged the cooler and towels to his specifications and adjusted the umbrella for maximum shade. When he pulled off his shirt, Gen bit back a groan of pleasure, seeing his bare torso in all its glory for the first time. "Are you coming?"

"Sure," Gen said, her heart going into overdrive as she stood up and unzipped her cover-up, aware of Zach standing just a step or two away, waiting for her.

Oh, she hoped he felt the same way looking at her as she did at the sight of those magnificent pecs and his firm, ridged abdomen.

She didn't look at him as she shrugged the sleeveless dress off her arms and stepped out of it, before bending to pick it up and fold it carefully.

Then, with the long strides she'd learned during her pageant days, she walked past him toward the surf.

He wasn't beside her as she ran the last few steps into the water before doing a shallow dive beneath an incoming wave.

When she came up and turned back toward the beach, wiping the salt water from her face, he was still standing where she'd left him. When their gazes collided, despite the distance between them a shiver of longing ran up her spine.

Then he was in motion, not running but following her with decisive, intentional strides. He didn't dive into the water, but kept wading until he was standing just inches from where she was bobbing in the water.

"You're trying to drive me bonkers, aren't you?"

It was little better than a growl, and her nipples tightened at his tone, while her core turned molten and needy.

"Is it working?" she asked, holding his gaze, trying to figure out if the gleam there was anger, annoyance or something else entirely.

"Yes," he snapped. "But this…" He waved his hand between them. "This is supposed to be make-believe."

She shrugged lightly. "It doesn't have to be. I'm horribly attracted to you, so if you want to change the rules, we can negotiate."

"Consider this my opening bid," he said, pulling her close, placing his hands on either side of her face and kissing her as though he'd never stop.

CHAPTER EIGHT

IT WAS A short trip to the beach.

Far shorter than Zach could ever have anticipated.

Having Gen in his arms in the water—her long legs wrapped around his waist, those beautiful breasts pressed against his chest—made him ravenous.

Almost unbearably so.

And the yummy little sounds she made as they kissed didn't help his growing need.

Eventually he had to gently disengage, and he held her until she found her footing in the water.

"Wow," she said, her tongue peeking out to touch her lower lips. "Oh, wow."

"Yeah," he said, watching her, wanting her so much it hurt.

She blinked a couple of times, then said, "Can we leave now?"

Her eagerness filled him with almost obscene pleasure and made him chuckle roughly.

"You're going to have to give me a few minutes. I can't walk out of the water like this."

She blushed and shook her head.

"Okay. Want to venture out a bit? Then we can at least say with all honesty that we went swimming."

He laughed and agreed, and they spent about a half hour in the surf, diving and swimming, keeping the conversation light. But beneath the chatter was the knowledge that when they left, it would be to go somewhere private and make love.

Even knowing the situation, he couldn't think of it as having sex. What he wanted from Gen felt so much more than a mechanical slaking of lust.

Although what, exactly, he wanted from the upcoming encounter—or her—he didn't dare consider too closely.

"Your place or mine?" she asked, after they left the water and packed up their kit.

"Mine, if that's okay with you?" He wanted her in his room, in his bed, with an almost primitive hunger.

And the smile she gave him made him want to grab her for another kiss, but he restrained himself.

They didn't speak much on the drive to his

house, or even when they pulled up and he parked.

In fact, the silence was thick, lying between them like smoke.

Then she said, "If you want to change your mind, this is the time to say so."

As if he were going to do any such thing.

"I'll say the same to you," he replied, not wanting to give her the out, but determined to do the right thing as best he could with desire riding him like a beast.

Her reply was to throw him a glance that smoldered with promise, open her door and step out.

Hastening to join her, he was by her side as they walked up the path to the back door. Puss meowed at them from the box he'd put out for her on the porch, but didn't come over to greet him the way she usually did. Maybe even the cat could feel the shimmering tension between them and wanted none of it.

When they got inside, she said, "I'd love to rinse off the salt."

"Sure," he replied, immediately imagining her under the shower, water sluicing over all that luscious flesh he'd seen and felt earlier, and his body hardened even more.

He led her along the corridor to the bathroom, stopping at the airing cupboard to get her a towel, suddenly aware of how threadbare they all were. His grandad hadn't replaced any of his linens after Gran died, and Zach felt self-conscious, wishing he'd thought to buy some new.

But Gen took it without hesitation, and with a thank-you.

As she followed him to the bathroom, he wondered what she'd think of the old fixtures and fittings. She'd only ever used the powder room upstairs, which was considerably newer than the rest of the house, having been put in twenty years before. Nothing else had been touched, he thought, since maybe the fifties. Perhaps even earlier than that.

"Here it is," he said, seeing the room as though through her eyes and fighting a wave of embarrassment.

The old cast-iron tub and stained sink. A toilet that belonged in the previous century by a number of decades. A vanity with wonky doors and peeling paint. The mirror so old some of the backing had come off, leaving it opaque in spots, brown-speckled in others.

From her own place, even though it was rented, he knew she was used to far more luxurious surroundings, and he wanted to apologize for the facilities.

Even while hating himself for the impulse.

He looked at her and found her staring back, not looking with distaste at the room.

Then she smiled, and whispered, "Wash my back?"

And suddenly the condition of the towel, the room, the house and even the entire blooming world could go hang.

No one had ever touched her body as gently as Zach did, with tenderness akin to reverence. Gen found herself stretching and almost preening beneath the intensity of his gaze, even as her body thrummed and tingled with ever-growing desire.

The sheer eroticism of standing under the fitful stream of water coming from the showerhead and having him slowly, carefully slick soap over her skin turned her knees to jelly. Need built inside, short-circuiting her brain, even though he only lightly touched her as he anointed each spot with the sudsy washcloth in his hand.

And she knew he wasn't unmoved by the experience. Not only was he marvelously erect, but his face was tight, the skin taut across the bones, giving him an almost predatory air, and his hands trembled, ever so slightly.

When she touched him, letting her fingers trace the hard muscles of arms and chest and abdomen, letting them fall to his thigh, the air hissed through his lips, as though each contact burned.

She knew how he felt. She was aflame, her flesh so sensitive each soft touch drove through nerves and blood and bone, until they all collected and collided in her core, driving her to lust-filled madness.

Yet, although strung tight as a bowstring, with urgency trying to take precedence—telling her to force him to hurry, do something to make him lose control—she let him take the lead. And the almost leisurely pace he set was, she knew instinctively, designed for maximum effect.

"Turn around."

His voice was raw, demanding, so in contrast to the tenderness of his ministrations it pulled a moan of pleasure from her throat.

She faced the tiled wall, felt the cloth slick over her shoulders and back, go lower, to her bottom. Then she heard him kneel, as he washed first one leg and then the other.

He pressed a kiss to her hip, and the spark of electricity firing out from that spot had her curling her fingers into the wall and almost made her legs give out.

If he didn't stop soon, she thought fuzzily,

she was going to have her way with him right here and now.

Before she could turn around and tell him so, he rose and pressed his chest against her back, his arms banding around her waist so his hands rested just below her breasts.

"You are the most gorgeous woman I've ever seen," he growled against her neck, before pressing his lips to her throat.

When his teeth scraped across her skin, and then his tongue followed, soothing the sharp, luscious pain, she had to grab his arms to keep on her feet.

"You're torturing me," she moaned, swiveling her hips against his hardness. "I want you—now."

But he wasn't finished with her.

Letting the cloth fall to the side of the tub, he slid his hands over her body—not gently now, but with the intent to excite already oversensitized skin—until she twisted and shook. With her head back on his shoulder, she whispered and sighed and mewled, trembling on the edge of orgasm.

Then he shifted, effortlessly lifting her into his arms before turning them both under the water and taking her lips in a kiss so hot, so deep, she felt it right down to her soul.

Still holding her aloft, he growled, "Turn off the water."

Leaning down, she did as he demanded, then he stepped out of the tub to carry her out of the bathroom.

"Don't you want to dry off?" she asked against his throat.

"No," he said, nudging a door open with his foot. "I like you wet."

It was on the tip of her tongue to tell him that was a good thing, but they were tumbling onto a bed, and he was kissing her again before the words could come out.

Zach made love as though he were on a mission, and his objective was to make her crazy with desire, then slake that thirst over and over again.

Not that she was passive. Once she realized he was holding himself back, while taking her to new, more thrilling heights with fingers, hands and lips, she decided to return the favor.

But when she tried to roll him over, so as to take control, he resisted, and those dark fathomless eyes snared hers.

"If you touch me, I won't last more than a minute."

His honesty moved her, made her want him even more.

"That would be okay," she said, although she

didn't try to wrest free. "I want to make you as happy as you're making me."

Those beautiful lips twisted into what she thought was meant to be a smile but looked more like a grimace.

"When I come, I want to be in you," he said. "I want to feel your body around mine."

The words, so raw and true, made her shiver, and she knew, then, she wanted the same thing.

"Yes," she whispered, lifting her head so her lips were against his. "Yes."

So he took her to the edge of another orgasm, and then went up on his knees to open a drawer by his bed and take out a condom.

Watching him roll it on, Gen shivered in anticipation.

She should be already satiated, but the need she felt was as sharp and hot as ever.

This, she realized, would be different.

Different from anything she'd experienced before, and not just because it was the first time making love with Zach.

But because it *was* Zach, who had already shown her more attention, tenderness and pleasure than any man ever had.

Acknowledging that brought a lick of fear, but it was overwhelmed by an intense wave of desire, which had her reaching for him, pulling him in close to her trembling body.

"Gently," he growled, taking his time, entering her body with all the care he'd shown when he bathed her. "Gently."

"No," she contradicted, tightening her legs around his hips, urging him as close as possible. Wanting—needing—him to let go. Wanting him ferociously, and wanting him as mindless and crazed as she felt. "Not gently, Zach. I need you, now."

He groaned, and, as though her words let loose something wild inside him, he withdrew, then thrust deep, and kept driving home until they both found release together.

CHAPTER NINE

ZACH SCROUNGED THROUGH the kitchen for something to make for lunch, completely distracted by the sight of Gen wandering around clad only in one of his T-shirts.

The shirt was big enough and long enough to cover all of her, but just knowing what lay beneath it, and that she was naked under it, made him hard all over again.

There was a part of him still in disbelief over the fact they'd made love. That she'd wanted him and shared her body with him.

Women like Genevieve Broussard didn't sleep with men like him, unless they had ulterior motives or were slumming. At least in his experience. Yet, try as he might, he couldn't figure out what possible reason she could have, other than finding him attractive.

He had already fallen in with her plan, and surely she knew him well enough by now to figure out he wouldn't back out on her. So there was no need to sweeten the pot, so to speak.

During one of their many nights talking, trying to get up to speed on each other's lives, she'd admitted what she called the sexual revolution had mostly passed her by.

"I've had a few long-term relationships," she'd said. "But I haven't had the kind of extensive experience some of my friends have. No hookups or really brief affairs. They never appealed to me."

Maybe this was Gen using him to catch up? To finally have a no-strings, no-expectations kind of relationship? Having a quick, hot affair with the sort of man she'd never consider for the long-term?

He slapped the bread he was carrying down onto the counter with a little more force than was strictly necessary, his eyes drawn unerringly back to her. She was standing in the doorway, looking out over the view. When she stretched, arms high above her head, it caused the shirt to ride up, revealing the toothsome curves of her bottom beneath the hem. He almost groaned aloud.

Clearing his throat was a necessity before he could ask, "Cheese toasties okay?"

"What're those?" she asked, turning and coming toward him. He had to tear his gaze away from the sway of her breasts, forcing himself to look her in the eyes.

The damned woman was far too gorgeous for his peace of mind.

"Cheese toasties. You know, cheese melted between toasted bread?"

"Oh, grilled cheese sandwiches." She grinned. "Sounds great."

Then, as he assembled the sandwiches, she came around behind him and put her arms around his waist. He hadn't bothered with a shirt, so when she leaned her cheek against his back, the silkiness of her skin had gooseflesh erupting across his torso.

"Is there anything I can do to help?"

Since she was rubbing her hands over his abs and then her lips across his back, all he could do was chuckle, and say, "Perhaps not be so much of a distraction, so I don't either cut myself or burn lunch?"

She giggled. "I guess I can do that."

Then, with a final kiss right between his shoulder blades, she sashayed over to the fridge to take out the pitcher of limeade he'd made that morning.

It was a wonder, he thought to himself, that his eyes didn't just drop out of his head and roll over to her, the way they were so intent on following her every move.

They ate at the table on the back veranda, since the front was in full sun and the day had turned unusually still, making it hotter than blazes. Just as they were finishing up, Zach's phone rang. He was going to ignore it, but Gen said, "Aren't you going to answer that? It might be important."

Nothing could be more important than spending time with her, but he stopped himself from saying so, and instead, went to answer in the kitchen, where he'd left his cell phone.

It was Kiah.

"Hey, cuz, where are you?"

"At home," he replied as Gen brought the plates and glasses into the kitchen. "What's up?"

"Nothing much," Kiah replied, but Zach thought he heard a strange tone in the other man's voice. "I'm off today and wondered if you wanted to come by. I have that Arsenal match on DVR, and I thought we could watch it together."

"Not today," Zach said, his gaze fixed on Gen as she put the dishes in the sink and started washing up. "Have a few things to take care of around here."

That earned him a saucy glance, and she nodded before pointing at herself and mouthing, *me*. Zach had to hold back a chuckle.

"Well…" Kiah drew out the word, making it three syllables instead of one. "You sure?"

"Yeah, man. I'll catch you another time."

"Okay," Kiah said, something suspiciously like amusement in his voice. "Behave yourself. Talk to you later."

As he hung up, Gen was drying her hands on a dishcloth, and her expression had him stalking over to pull her close.

"I was just thinking… You know what you need here?" she asked, twining her arms around his neck.

"What?" He bent to find the spot just behind her ear with his lips, feeling her shiver as he placed a kiss there.

"A bed on the veranda."

Lifting his head, he gave her a curious look. "A bed? Why?"

"I think it would be beyond amazing to make love with you out there as the sun is going down."

She was thinking about places and settings to make love with him.

Somehow hearing her say that had a warm spot opening up in his chest and stole his breath for a minute.

"I'll bear that in mind when I'm redecorating," he replied, his voice a little rough. "Just for you. In the meantime, may I recommend the living room sofa, which is very, very comfortable and also has an amazing view?"

"Mmmm," she said, which he took for agreement when she eased out of his arms and started leading him that way. "Let's check it out."

But Gen had a plan, and Zach soon found himself seated on the sofa, with her kneeling between his spread thighs, doing things to him that he was sure were illegal in several places.

She teased him, taking him so close to orgasm he was sure he couldn't hold back a second more, before easing him back down to where the desire was once more bearable. If only just.

When she stood up and took the shirt off over her head, he growled low in his throat at the sight of her gorgeous body, his fingertips tingling with the need to touch her everywhere.

Straddling his thighs, she said, "We should have brought a condom."

He held on to her waist and flipped her over onto her back in one swift motion, eliciting a squeak of surprise from her.

"I'll go get one in a minute," he said, his lips already around one dark, peaked nipple.

He paid her back for the delicious torment she'd wreaked on him, until she was panting and pleading.

Rolling off the couch was torture, especially when he looked down and saw the glazed, desire-struck expression on her face.

"I'll be right back," he said, unable to resist stroking a hand along one of her long, trembling, outflung legs. "Stay right there."

Taking the front steps from the living room to the floor below got him to his bedroom in a thrice. By the time he'd fetched a condom from the drawer, he heard a sound behind him and turned to see Gen standing in the doorway.

"I couldn't wait," she whispered, as though confessing something slightly shameful. "I want you so very, very much."

Tearing open the packet, he rolled on the prophylactic while walking back across the room to her, already as desperate as she was to be joined together again.

Lifting her, he was about to carry her to the bed, but she put her legs around his waist and wriggled into position with a little cry of pleasure, engulfing him where they stood. So he sidestepped, placing her back to the wall, and tried to hold on to control while she used her thigh muscles and the leverage of her arms around his shoulders to rise and fall.

"Oh!" she cried, her head back against the wall, baring her throat to his ravaging mouth. "Oh, oh, *oh*."

It was too much, and not enough.

Mindless with lust, he dropped his hands to that delectable bottom and took over, driving into her as she egged him on, telling him to go faster, harder, *yes, yes, yes.*

When she came, she arched against the wall, shifting the angle of penetration, and Zach heard himself shout, as bursts of colored lights flashed behind his eyelids, and the top of his head seemed to lift off.

He was still trying to catch his breath, using all his energy to hold her up, locking his knees to keep standing, when she whispered, "Was that a car?"

"What?" he mumbled. "I didn't—"

Then came the unmistakable sound of car doors slamming and voices coming up the path.

The back door was flung open, and a male voice called out, "Zachary? Where are you?"

And as he met Gen's wide gaze, which seemed caught somewhere between amusement and horror, all he could do was whisper, "That's my dad!"

She had to give Zach credit for not dropping her, despite his shock and being galvanized into action. Instead, he carried her quickly to the bed and lowered her onto it, as they heard voices— including one she figured was his mother's— and footsteps going up to the kitchen along the back stairs.

"I thought you said they'd never surprise you

like this," she whispered, trying to quell the urge to go into hysterics.

"I never thought they would," he replied, looking around a little wildly. "Where the hell are my shorts?"

"In the living room," she said, stifling a snort of laughter. Then she remembered her bathing suit and cover-up were in the bathroom and bounced off the bed, saying, "Coo-calloo-calloo, I have to get my clothes."

Zach was pulling on another pair of shorts, and said, "Stay here. I'll get them."

He was gone and back quickly, wiping his face with a towel. He handed her the still-damp bathing suit and cover-up, before heading for the door again, pulling a shirt on over his head.

Then he paused with his hand on the latch and looked back at her with a baffled, half-angry expression.

"I'm sorry about this, Gen. I've dropped us both in the soup."

He looked so genuinely concerned, her heart turned over. Caught in the act of untangling her bikini top, she dropped it on the bed and went to him. Putting her hands on his shoulders, she smiled before giving him a soft, quick kiss.

"Nothing to apologize for. And if there is anything, it should be me saying sorry. I started this whole thing, remember?"

"Yeah, but—"

She kissed him again, "Go see your family, before someone comes looking for you and catches me buck naked."

"Come up when you feel like, yeah?" he said, his gaze still shadowed.

"It's the least I can do," she replied, giving him a grin, although her heart was hammering. "Since I seduced you into this position."

And that, at least, made him smile in return.

"Seduction by you is always welcome," he said.

Then he was gone.

In no more than a minute, she heard cries of delighted greeting, and the general hubbub of a successful surprise.

After pulling on her clothes, she made a quick trip to the bathroom, where she looked at herself in the mirror with horrified amusement.

Her hair, although short and usually easy to maintain, was at its unruliest best because of the seawater, ad hoc shower, and, well, several rolls in the hay. Using Zach's brush, she got it somewhat under control, but although she washed her face with cold water, there was no washing off the beard burn on her cheeks.

If she had her own car, she'd be tempted to beat a hasty retreat, but since that wasn't an option, she decided bold insouciance was the next best thing. But first, a quick trip up the front steps to see if she could retrieve Zach's clothes from the living room unseen.

She was in luck, as everyone was on the veranda and out of view, so with shorts and shirt in hand, she slipped back downstairs to put them in Zach's room.

About to go back out, she paused, smiling, as memories of their time together cycled through her head.

She had some answers now. Zach had freckles on his face, but only a smattering anywhere else, and he was an even better lover than he was kisser. He'd fulfilled her every fantasy and left her greedy for more.

But now she had to face the music upstairs, and she couldn't help wondering what his parents would make of her, whether they'd think her good enough for their son. It wasn't that she lacked confidence, really, but just that she now knew exactly how fine a man he was. His parents should want him to have the best, not a lopsided ex–beauty queen who was always doing crazy things.

Although, the crazy stuff she'd done—coming to St. Eustace almost on a whim, asking him to pretend to be her lover—had led her right to this place, so they weren't that insane, really.

Realizing she was shilly-shallying, she forced

herself to leave the room and go along the corridor to the back stairs.

Going up and then through the kitchen, she took a deep breath to quell her vibrating nerves. Plastering a million-kilowatt smile on her face, she went through the door and out onto the veranda.

"Hi, everyone," she said, taking in the surprised expressions on Zach's parents' faces, as they turned at the sound of her voice. But it was the double take Kiah gave her that was almost her undoing, and she had to fight laughter as she asked, "Can I get you all something to drink?"

CHAPTER TEN

"A SURGEON, EH, son?"

Zach and his father were walking in the garden, making use of the last rays of the sun, Dad checking on the progress his son and Mass Alex had made on clearing the land.

Not sure what his father's placid-sounding question really meant, Zach just made a noncommittal sound in the back of his throat.

"She's nice enough," the older man continued. "Friendly. Real pretty too."

"She is," Zach agreed, refusing to elaborate any further.

"What happened to her face? Car accident? Stroke?"

"No, Dad. She had a condition called Bell's palsy. It damaged some of the nerves in her face."

"Still look nice, though," his father said. "Never let it stop her either, eh?" Then, as he appeared to examine an allamanda plant beside the driveway, he added again, "A surgeon."

Zach knew what his father was getting at, and he wished he could contradict his father's assumptions.

His dad described himself as a simple man, with simple tastes and needs. Zach understood. He thought of himself the same way. Anything too fancy—or *stoosh*, as his father liked to say, using a word picked up from one of his Jamaican friends—held no appeal.

Usually.

Gen was nice and kind and easy to be around, but there was no getting around the fact that she was, in the final analysis, fancy.

From the way she spoke, with that sweet drawl, to how she carried herself, to the lifestyle she was accustomed to, she was definitely out of Zach's league.

Miles out of it.

Very much as Moira had turned out to be, although Moira never treated his parents with the warmth Gen had earlier.

She'd stepped out onto the veranda like a queen and proceeded to show exactly why the best defense was a good offence. It was pretty obvious what they'd been up to when his parents and Kiah arrived, but Gen handled the whole affair as though everyone had dropped by for tea. And not unexpectedly either.

She'd brought out juice and water, sprinkling good humor and sunshine on all of them as she did.

And everyone just went along with it, although Kiah had looked dumbstruck.

Now that he thought about it, Kiah hadn't mentioned anything to Zach about hearing the rumors about them, nor about Mina clueing him in to what was happening. Or maybe she had, and his reaction was to the newly intimate nature of Zach and Gen's relationship.

Mum had just looked on, seemingly gobsmacked. But when Gen engaged her in conversation, they got on like a house on fire, chatting away about all sorts of topics, from their flight to the weather, to knitting of all things. Everything and nothing really.

Kiah, being in the know about his parents' arrival, had made reservations at a restaurant for the Lewin family to have an early dinner, but when Zach invited Gen, she refused.

"No, thank you," she said with one of those brilliant smiles she wielded with such expertise. "I'm not dressed to go out. Besides, it'll be nice for your parents to have you to themselves on their first evening here."

"I'll drop Gen home," Kiah said. "You're up on Cottage Road, right?"

"I am," she replied, as serene as a forest pool, even though she may well have suspected she was in for a grilling from his cousin. "And thanks. That'll work out well."

At dinner, Mum, in her forthright way, had said, "How serious are you two, Zachary?"

"Not very," he said, even though, for him, things had become infinitely more serious that day. "We enjoy each other's company."

Mum gave him a long look, but didn't say anything more about Gen.

"Let's go for a walk on Coconut Beach," Dad said as they were leaving the restaurant. "I want to watch the sunset with you, wifey."

"Not on your Nellie," Mum replied. "I'm already half-dead from jet lag and just want to put my feet up and have a cuppa. I don't mind staying up so I don't wake up at three in the morning, but I'm not tramping for miles with you in the sand tonight."

"Just as well," Dad said with one of the smiles he reserved just for her. He rubbed his chest as he continued, "I'm a little beat myself."

But even after saying so, he'd insisted on a walk around the garden after they got back.

Zach noticed his father rubbing his chest again, just below the sternum.

"All right there, Dad?"

"Hmm?"

"You're rubbing your chest. Are you in pain?"

"No. No. Just a little indigestion. Airport and then plane food, and being locked up in a shoe-box to fly over the ocean would give anybody gas."

Zach was going to tell him to let him know if the pain got worse, but Dad forestalled him by pointing to where Puss followed them, stopping to look for lizards or maybe smell the flowers.

"And since when you get a cat? You always used to want a dog, when you was young."

Zach shrugged. "It just turned up one day, out of the blue. And now she doesn't want to leave, probably because I feed her," he admitted.

Dad smiled. "Sometimes the best things in life come out of the blue, and it's best to hold on to them."

Zach smiled back, the words settling over him like a warm arm around his shoulders.

"Come on up and have some tea, Dad. It should be strong enough for you now."

"Yeah," his father grumbled. "Not like that dishwater your mother always drinks."

They laughed together at the long-standing family joke as they walked back up the drive-way, and Zach realized he was happy in a way he hadn't been for a long, long time.

The only thing that could make it more perfect was if Gen were there to share it all.

Yet, he knew he shouldn't even entertain such a thought, much less the attendant longing. Genevieve would be through with him as soon as her mother left.

He was sure of that.

Gen put down her phone on the coffee table and glared at it.

"Coo-calloo-calloo," she said on a huff of expelled air. "It never rains but it pours."

First making love with Zach, then his parents arriving totally unexpectedly, and now…

The phone rang again, and when she saw Zach's name come up, she grabbed it and hit the Accept icon.

"Hey." His low, soft greeting melted her, deep inside. "Just checking in with you."

"I'm fine. Everything going well there?" she asked, lying back on the couch and closing her eyes, just so happy to hear his voice and to know that, even with his parents there, he'd thought of her.

"Yes. They're having tea, trying to stay awake a bit more before they go to bed, although it's obvious they're exhausted."

"Poor souls. Jetlag is a beast."

"That it is."

Taking a deep breath, she said, "I got some news this evening."

"Oh?"

"My mother isn't coming in five days. She'll be here the day after tomorrow."

There was silence on the other end of the line, and then Zach laughed.

Gen huffed, even though the sound of his amusement made her smile too. "If you *dare* to make any smart comments about knowing where my impulsive behavior comes from, I'll be highly upset."

"The thought never crossed my mind," he replied between chuckles. "Why the sudden change?"

"Apparently Daddy's been asked to attend a conference in Addis Ababa, and there's no way Mom would miss the opportunity to go with him. She's fascinated by African cultures, and she's never been to Ethiopia. The conference starts the day before she would have been flying back to the States, so she's moved her trip here up. Shortened it by a few days too. She's just coming for a week now."

After a moment, Zach said, "Changing her flight like that must have cost her a pretty penny."

Gen chuckled. "You haven't met my mom yet, but when you do, you'll realize that by the time she was finished with them, the airline probably gave her money off, if not a free flight for the pleasure of helping her out."

"Ahh, so that's where you get your powers of persuasion."

She ignored that comment, not wanting to go down that road. After all, that was partially what brought them to this point.

Okay, was absolutely what brought them to this point.

"The main thing is—we're going to have both your parents *and* my mom here, all at the same time."

"The plot thickens."

Could it get any thicker? Gen doubted it.

"Right? I'm so sorry I got you into this. I never had any intention of getting your family involved. I hope it doesn't cause you any problems."

"They're curious about you, but I told them we weren't seriously involved, just enjoying each other, and I think they're okay with that."

He was right, of course, so his words shouldn't hurt the way they did.

But all she said in reply was, "Good." Then a question she'd been pondering all day popped back into her mind. "So, what made your parents decide to come to see you right now?"

"I asked them the same thing, and they said

the company Dad works for changed hands, and the new management wanted to clear up all the old, accrued holiday time. They didn't want him to take it all, because then he'd be off the job for months, but offered him three weeks off, plus compensation for the rest."

"So, he ended up with a bit of a windfall, as well as time off."

"Yeah."

"And spent some of it to come see you. That's really nice."

"I'm not sure if my being here was the primary motivation. He's been asking me about the repairs to the house, so I'm guessing he wanted to check up on that too."

"Really?" She infused laughter into her voice. "Silly rabbit, your mom couldn't stop looking at and touching you. They missed you and wanted to see you."

He grunted, the sound so typically male and noncommittal she couldn't help giggling. He didn't comment on her amusement, as though not wanting to get into it.

Instead, he said, "Kiah, that sneaky fellow, somehow got me some time off for while the parents are here, so I'll be taking them around. Do you think your mum would get along with my parents?" He said the last part slowly, as though reluctant to ask.

"My mom gets along with everybody." Then, on further consideration, Gen had to add, "Well, my mom tries to get to know everyone she meets, which drives my father crazy. He's constantly asking her if she *has* to talk to people in the grocery store or restaurant or wherever they are. The thing is, though, people either really like her or can't stand her, so we'll just have to wait and see."

"It would be good if they do get along," he said, still with that hesitation in his tone. "Then we could take them around, all at the same time. Unless you want to spend time alone with your mum."

"That would be great, making one thing of it," she agreed, although she couldn't help wondering what made him sound so unsure. "Do you think your parents would like that?"

"I know Dad would love to have someone new to show off the island to," Zach said, clearly amused now. "And Mum probably would like the company too."

"Perfect," she said, infusing both enthusiasm and surety into her tone. "As soon as Mom gets here, we'll get them all together and see how it shakes out. Agreed?"

"Agreed," he echoed. Then he said, "I hope Kiah didn't give you too much of an interrogation when he drove you home?"

Gen chuckled, but a wave of heat rose into her face, making her glad he wasn't there to see it.

"It wasn't too bad," she lied, not wanting to cause any friction between Zach and his cousin. "He was just curious, because Mina had told him, no matter what else he heard, we weren't really involved. Clearly, he realized we're more involved than they expected."

If by *involved*, she meant having wild, amazing, heart-stopping sex all around his house, and her really, really, wanting to go back for more.

Zach was quiet for a second, and she wondered if he was thinking about what had happened earlier too.

He cleared his throat, then said, "Hmm, I was afraid he'd give you a hard time."

Kiah, like his wife, Mina, had read Gen the riot act and warned her not to hurt Zach. To which she'd rebutted that, since they weren't serious about each other, there was nothing for Zach to be hurt by.

At the rate they were going, though, Gen realized she might be endangering her own heart.

Yet, what she really wanted to know was what had happened to make everyone so protective of Zach?

"No, it was fine."

There was the sound of voices behind him, and a muffled conversation. When he came back to her, he said, "I have to go. But before we hang up—you're off tomorrow, aren't you? Want to come and toodle around with us? I don't know what they'll want to do yet, but you're more than welcome…"

"I wish I could," she replied, genuinely regretful. "But now that my mom's coming sooner than I expected, I'm going to have to clean and figure out some time off too."

"Understood." She wished he sounded upset, but his tone gave nothing away. "Well, 'night, then."

"Yes, 'night. Sleep well."

Just as she was about to lower the phone, he said her name, and a little tremor ran up her spine at the sound.

"Yes? I'm still here."

"I wish you were *here*, with me, right now."

"I do too," she said, her heart hammering, her body reacting as though she were.

"Talk to you tomorrow," he said, and then he was gone, leaving her clutching the phone like a hormonal teenager, considering whether she should call him right back. Get him to say explicitly what he'd do to her, if she were there.

That would be beyond puerile. So, placing the phone back on the coffee table, she resolutely got up to finish tidying the kitchen, which was what she'd been doing when her mom called.

But she couldn't stop her heart giving a little kick when she came back out and saw the message from Zach.

I want you…

CHAPTER ELEVEN

THE FOLLOWING DAY was a whirlwind of cleaning and shopping.

Gen stopped by the hospital on the way to the store to speak to Director Hamilton about the possibility of time off.

"I hate to drop this on you so abruptly, Director, but my mother is a force of nature who defies resistance."

She was profoundly appreciative of the director's laughter-filled understanding.

"I'll be at work tomorrow, as scheduled," she assured him. "And I'd be happy to be on call while I'm off, if you need me to be. And if I plan to take Mom to the other end of the island, or anything like that, I can let you know beforehand, if that will help."

"I think we can manage without you for a few days, but it would put my mind to rest to know you're available, if necessary. John Goulding will be off the island for a few days during that time," he said, still chuckling. "Enjoy your visit with her. Oh, and I guess with Zachary's parents too," he added smoothly, but it was impossible not to notice the speculative look in his eyes. "Things going well between you?"

"Ah, yes. Very nicely." Talk about being put on the spot! "But I hope you realize that whatever relationship Zach and I have has no bearing on our performance here in the hospital?"

His lips were still smiling, but his eyes suddenly weren't. "I would expect no less, and I'm glad to say I've heard no complaints."

After that, he changed the subject, saying once more how much he hoped she enjoyed the time with her mother, as he rose and escorted her to the door of his office.

By the end of the day, she was tired, having scrubbed the townhouse from top to bottom and done some meal prep for the week ahead. Mom was usually a ball of energy and would probably want to go out to start experiencing the island immediately. But Gen wanted to be ready if next evening she ended up cooking at home.

She showered. Then she went into the kitchen and was trying to work up the enthusiasm to fix a meal when her phone rang.

That had her running back into the living room, and her heart did a little flip when she realized it was Zach.

"Hi," she said, hoping he'd put the breathiness of her tone down to something other than her excitement at hearing his voice. "What's going on? How was the day? What did you do?"

He chuckled. "Slow down, Lewis Hamilton. Before you pepper me with questions, I have one for you. Would you like to come out and have dinner with us? Mum's just getting changed, and then we'll leave. But we can pick you up on the way."

"I'd love to," she said, grinning like crazy. "I'll just need to put on something other than sweats."

Mr. Lewin wanted fried flying fish, so they went to one of the restaurants along a rocky part of the coast that was patronized by locals. It was fairly quiet, and they had the patio mostly to themselves.

Mrs. Lewin had no interest in the local delicacy, but muttered to Gen, "Thank goodness you can always find chicken on a menu. I definitely don't share Hezekiah's obsession with that dish."

"Do you know that Barbados and Trinidad almost went to war over flying fish?" Mr. Lewin asked, drawing groans from both his wife and son.

"Yes, Dad. You've told us a thousand times."

Mr. Lewin's lips twisted to the side as he shot his son a laughing look.

"But I didn't know," Gen said, genuinely curious. "How did that happen?"

"Don't encourage him, dear," Mrs. Lewin said. "Once he gets started on these stories, we can't get him to stop."

"Well," Mr. Lewin began, "cou-cou and flying fish is Barbados's national dish, you know, but the fish started migrating out of Bajan waters—"

"Now you've done it," Zach groaned, but the look he sent Gen was so tender and sweet, she had no regrets.

Mr. Lewin told more stories after that one, but his voice got hoarse, and he stopped just before their meals arrived at the table.

As they were eating, Mrs. Lewin asked Gen, "Are you looking forward to seeing your mum?"

"I am," she replied. "Although she put me on the spot by changing her plans so suddenly. Luckily the director was understanding, and I got the time off I wanted."

"Does she work?" Mrs. Lewin asked next.

"Yes. She's an economics professor, so she's on summer break just now."

There was no mistaking the glance shared between Zach's parents on hearing that, but Mrs.

Lewin only looked mildly curious as she asked, "And what does your father do?"

There was no need to feel self-conscious, but something about the way Zach was gazing fixedly at his plate made the back of Gen's neck prickle as she replied, "He's an astrophysicist."

"Oh, my." Mrs. Lewin's eyes widened for an instant, and then she smiled. "How interesting."

Nothing more was said, as Zach changed the subject to what they had planned for the next day. But later, as Gen got ready for bed, the sense of unease she'd felt at that moment came back.

The atmosphere had seemed to change ever so slightly thereafter, and the entire experience left her on edge.

Her workday seemed never-ending, with several scheduled operations, plus an emergency stabbing victim, who was brought in just as Gen was preparing to start a gall bladder removal. The severity of the penetrating injuries the young man suffered kept her in the OR until not long before she was scheduled to leave.

When she finally was able to check her phone, there was a message from Zach, asking her to call him when she got the time.

She felt a frisson of apprehension as she remembered the somewhat strained atmosphere the evening before.

Had he decided not to come to the airport with her to pick up her mother? Or even intended to tell her he wanted to back out of her plan?

Thinking those things made her not want to call, but she ducked into an empty room and did anyway.

"Hello. How's your day going?"

There was no hint of anything untoward in his voice, and her shoulders relaxed as she smiled.

"Good, so far. I just have a few things to tie up here, and then I'm heading home. How was *your* day? Did you take your parents to the market, like your dad wanted?"

He groaned. "Yeah. He insisted on walking the entire building and bought a whack of stuff we don't need, including veg I have growing in the garden. It was so hot, it tired both of them out, so they came back and napped. But now he's awake again and in the kitchen. He decided he wants to make curry chicken for dinner."

Gen laughed. "Your dad's amazing. I love him."

Zach snorted. "You can love him, because you didn't have to trail after him all over Port Michael Market while he stopped to talk to every vendor. And you didn't have to carry loads of produce for him too. I felt like a Sherpa."

Still giggling at his griping, she asked, "What did you do while they napped?"

"Puttered around," he replied, his voice suddenly deeper, silkier. "Thinking about you, wishing you were here, so we could…nap… together."

Her breath caught, and her heart did a little flip as heat fired out from her core to all points north, south, east and west.

Especially south, as she remembered the thrill of him holding her aloft, the two of them moving together.

She cleared her throat. "I would have liked that too," she said as demurely as she could while thinking about holding him down and doing all things naughty to him. "Although, if I had my way, there wouldn't be much actual napping involved."

The sound he made had a shiver of longing traveling up her spine and made her already warm face grow hot.

"Exactly."

Oh, how she loved that gravelly growl that invaded his voice when he was turned on.

"It's a shame," she said, letting her voice drop almost to a whisper. "Such a shame that with all our family around, there won't be much chance for…napping."

"I think we should try to make time, don't you?"

"Yes…"

Gosh, she sounded as needy as she felt.

"What time are you leaving there?"

"In about ten minutes, give or take."

"I'll meet you at home, yeah? So we can… nap…before picking your mum up at the airport?"

"Yeah," she echoed, her legs already trembling at the thought. "Definitely."

"See you in a few," he replied, his voice rumbling through the phone and into her veins.

It was not surprising that she had to exert Herculean effort to concentrate on what she needed to get done before she could leave the hospital.

Equally unsurprising was that she had to remind herself not to speed as she drove home twenty minutes later.

Turning into the parking lot, her heart skipped a beat when she saw Zach's car already in her visitor's spot, and him leaning against the driver's door.

After she parked and then got out, she knew she should greet him, say something, but her heart was thundering, and her knees threatened to give out, they were so weak.

He walked across to her, but didn't speak either, just put his hand on the small of her back to guide her up the path to her door, and the heat of his palm, even through her clothing, was intense.

It took her two tries to get her key into the lock, and then they were inside, with Zach shutting the door decisively behind them as she turned to face him in the hallway.

But he stayed where he was, his gaze fixed to her face as he said, "I hardly slept last night, thinking about you."

She nodded, admitting, "I had the same problem."

"This isn't going the way we planned, is it?"

Suddenly, her palms started sweating, and a cold space opened up in her belly.

"No, it isn't. Is it becoming...an issue for you?"

He seemed to consider her question, and from her peripheral vision, she saw his fingers clench and then relax, twice.

"I don't know," he replied with characteristic honesty. "Half of me wants to just go with it and not think. The other bit, though, is trying to make me consider if we are getting in too deep."

By *we* she assumed he meant *you*, and she

lifted her chin, determined to let him know she wouldn't try to hang on to him when it was all over.

No matter how much she might want to.

"We set the parameters before we got into this, and although we've taken it further than we first agreed, I don't see why we can't just enjoy what we have. No need to stress about it, is there?"

He didn't reply, just took the one stride necessary to reach her and pull her into his arms.

Then, *oh*, there was no more time to think or to worry, because the blazing passion between them instantly ignited and all she could do was feel and yearn.

They moved awkwardly up the stairs and toward her room, pausing so she could toe off her shoes and shedding garments as they went. Their fitful, almost shambling progress would have been funny if the need wasn't so desperate, the desire so intense.

"I should shower..."

"No," he growled against her throat as they tumbled onto her bed. "I have to touch you. Taste you. Now."

His frank expression of craving only pushed her own higher, and it took only a few light touches to push her over the edge into ecstasy.

Yet, he didn't stop, but feasted on her body

as though starved and desperate, until she cried out again, the sound echoing through the room.

"More," she demanded, twisting so they tangled together in an erotic dance and she could touch him, bring him to the same place of longing she already inhabited.

Eventually, when waiting was no longer an option, she took the condom from his hand and rolled it on. Looking up, she saw that taut, ferocious expression on his face and knew he wanted her just as urgently as she did him.

"I want to watch you," she told him, pushing him onto his back so as to straddle his muscular thighs. His groan of acquiescence sent additional heat through her body.

She took him deep, watched as his back arched, the muscles in his neck and shoulders flexed and his eyes closed. He was clutching the sheets in fisted hands as though trying to let her have her way without interference and finding it difficult to do.

As she began to move, his hips powered up to meet hers, and her body tightened, strained, from the delicious sensations firing through her system. When his hands came up to caress her breasts, Gen shuddered, a new layer added to her pleasure.

But she didn't want it to end too soon. Maybe never, ever wanted it to end, really. She slowed, taking her time to swivel and rock against him, and although his strong hands fell to her hips as though wanting to take charge, he didn't try to force her to go faster.

Then his eyelids rose, and the fierceness of his gaze almost undid her.

"Gen. *Gen*," was all he said, his voice a low, needy rasp, but it was all the encouragement necessary.

Giving him what he wanted, she rode him hard and fast, and in doing so was catapulted into orgasm first, her fingers digging into his abs as she wrung every last drop of pleasure from the moment. And the intensity of that pleasure was deepened by the sensation of Zach pulsing inside her and hearing him cry out as he found his own release.

CHAPTER TWELVE

THEY WERE ALMOST late to the airport, but when they arrived and saw passengers already coming out of customs there was no sign of Gen's mother. So they found a spot across from the exit to wait.

Standing beside Gen, seeing some of the passing men—and a few women too—give her the once-over brought out a strange mix of emotions in Zach.

Pride, because she was so amazingly beautiful, but also something akin to possessiveness. When he took her hand, he hoped she thought it was just so her mum would think they looked like a couple, but in reality he was in his own subtle way staking a claim.

He rubbed her knuckles with his thumb.

"Doing all right?" he asked.

"Yes. More than fine." She gave him a sideways glance, redolent with memories of the time just spent in her bed, and her lips quirked with a secretive smile. "Just wondering where Mom is. Knowing her, she's probably chatting with someone and will be the last off the plane."

Zach chuckled. "I'm beginning to think I'm going to start recognizing a lot of you in your mum."

For which he got a glare, although she couldn't keep it up for long.

"Unfortunately, quite possibly so," she answered, shaking her head, smiling once more.

Even holding her hand didn't seem enough, so he let go and put his arm around her shoulders instead, and her snuggling against him with a sigh brought a rush of happiness.

This sense of belonging and possessiveness, he knew, was something he was going to have to contain and stamp out. And the sooner the better.

Gen had made it clear that their relationship hadn't really changed despite their new intimacy. That, in her mind, they were still playacting, although the lines between theater and reality had blurred.

For Zach they hadn't blurred but shifted. He'd forgotten to think of her as a make-believe lover and allowed the attraction and admiration he felt to overtake his better judgment, and he wasn't sure what to do about any of it.

What he knew for a certainty was that as long

as Gen was willing to be in his life or to share herself with him intimately, he'd welcome her with open arms.

He didn't want to think about the time when it would be all over and tried to convince himself that, like her, he'd just enjoy what they had for as long as it lasted.

"There she is," Gen said, breaking him out of his twisty-turny thoughts.

Focusing on the exit from customs, he saw a lady waving, a huge smile on her face. Shorter than Gen and with an ample figure, Mrs. Broussard was dressed in a casual light yellow dress that swept her ankles as she walked, accessorized with a necklace made of big blue beads, and matching earrings. There were bangles on her wrist that he could hear jingling even from where they stood, and her hair was braided in an elaborate cane row design. On her arm she carried an enormous multicolored bag, which reminded him of the tote Gen usually had with her when she went out.

There was something unmistakably elegant in her outfit and carriage, and Zach couldn't help wondering what his parents—both so salt of the earth—would make of Mrs. Broussard.

Gen stepped out from under his arm and walked to meet her mother, and Zach followed a little behind, giving them a chance to greet each other without interfering.

As soon as the gap closed enough, Mrs. Broussard let go of her rolling suitcase and opened her arms.

"ViVi!" she cried, before enveloping her daughter in a huge hug, rocking her from side to side. "Oh, my baby!"

By the time she let go, Zach was close enough to see Gen was blushing, but there was also a beaming smile on her face, and the love between the two women was patently obvious.

"Wow, Mom. I think any cred I might have built up here as a badass surgeon just went out the window."

"Nonsense," her mother replied, in a tone that brooked no argument. "No matter how old you are, you're still my baby, and I don't care who knows it."

Before Gen could answer, Mrs. Broussard turned her light brown gaze his way and said, "And you must be Zachary."

He hardly had time to open his mouth before he, too, was grabbed and hugged tightly and then had a kiss placed on either cheek.

Holding his shoulders, she gave his face a comprehensive once-over and then nodded.

"You're as handsome as ViVi said you were. It's so nice to finally meet you."

"It's a pleasure to meet you too, Mrs. Broussard," he replied, smiling back at her, thinking that although they didn't look very much alike, Gen and her mother certainly had some of the same appealing traits.

"Call me Marielle," she said, her eyes twinkling as she sent a quick sideways glance at Gen. "Or Mom, if you prefer."

"Mom..."

There was a definite warning in the word, but Mrs. Broussard swept right past it, as if she hadn't heard her daughter.

Linking her arm through Gen's, she headed for the exit. "So, where are we going when we leave here? Can I buy you both dinner? I didn't eat on the plane. That food always makes me feel queasy."

"I thought you might like to rest after your flight," Gen interposed, while Zach took ahold of the suitcase and caught up to them at the door.

"Nonsense," came the tart reply. "What is there to do on a plane but rest?"

"My dad's cooking a curry at our place," Zach said as they walked toward where the car was parked. "And he told me to invite you if you'd like to come."

"What a lovely, gracious invitation." Marielle Broussard turned her beaming smile his way, and that was when he truly saw the resemblance between mother and daughter. "I'd love to meet your parents, Zachary."

"Why don't you drop us off at my place, Zach?" Gen had the slightly cornered look of a woman who'd lost control of her life and was trying to claw it back, and it made him want to chuckle. "That way we can drive up and save you having to drive us back later."

"I don't mind at all taking you home after dinner." Now at the car, he left the suitcase beside the boot and opened the back door for Mrs. Broussard. "It's not a problem at all." As he closed the door behind her mother and then reached to open Gen's, he whispered, *"ViVi."*

"Don't you start," she said, wrinkling her nose and keeping him from opening the door by leaning against it. "With an appropriate last name, I'd sound like a stripper."

He shrugged, raising his eyebrows suggestively. "Maybe that's why I like it?"

"Oh, you…"

But she was laughing as she moved so he could pull open her door and as she slid into the front seat.

Jumping from subject to subject was another trait Gen and her mother shared, and Zach found himself mostly excluded from the conversation as Gen's mother brought her up to speed on family news.

As they turned up into the hills behind Port Michael, Marielle Broussard exclaimed, "What a beautiful place. So unspoiled and green. No wonder you won't discuss coming home, ViVi."

"It is lovely here," Gen replied in that serene voice she used when she had no intention of elaborating further.

"And, I suppose now you've met Zachary..."

"Mom."

No mistaking the quelling tone there, and Zach couldn't help smiling to himself when he heard her mother hum a little tune from the back seat, as though totally unmoved.

When they got to the house, there were a couple of cars already there, and Zach wasn't sure whether to be relieved or annoyed. Trust Dad to turn a quiet dinner into a jamboree.

"That's Kiah's car, isn't it?" Gen asked. "But I don't recognize the other one."

"Probably one of Dad's childhood friends," he replied, glancing at Gen to see her reaction.

"Lovely," she said, sending him a smile. "The more the merrier, right?"

"Yeah," he said, although he wasn't at all sure he agreed.

"I love a party," Mrs. Broussard said happily

from the back seat as Zach parked. "One of my favorite things."

Gen chuckled and shook her head. "My mom's a social butterfly," she explained. "Just keep her away from the wine, or she'll be dancing in the moonlight in the garden."

"Genevieve!"

At the horrified exclamation, Gen said, "Sorry, Mom. Too much information?"

"Don't worry, Mrs. B," Zach said as he was opening his door. "My mum might just be dancing with you. She may be a good Scottish lass, but she's a lightweight when it comes to wine."

And they were all still laughing together as they made their way inside and upstairs.

Bless Mr. Lewin, Gen thought a couple of hours later.

"Well, your mum told me I'd cooked too much food, and I thought I'd just invite a few more people to help us eat it," he told Zach when they went inside.

And in doing so, he turned what could have been a stilted, awkward first meeting of their parents into a fun, laughter-filled evening.

Not that Gen was worried, per se, about how they'd get on with her mother. Just that Mom was—well—so extroverted, she could seem a bit overbearing to those who didn't know her.

Having a room full of people let her shine without any one person having to weather the brunt of her attention.

However, she greeted each and every person as though they were long-lost relatives, and Gen couldn't help wondering how Mr. and Mrs. Lewin, in particular, felt about being grabbed, hugged and kissed.

Kiah and Mina were indeed there, as well as Kiah's grandmother Miss Pearl, and another couple, Mr. and Mrs. Morris, whom Mr. Lewin had known since school days.

"Where's Charm?" Zach asked Mina as he hugged her and kissed her cheek. "And those two young ruffians of yours?"

"Charm's babysitting for us so Miss Pearl could come along too, without any of us having to constantly keep an eye on them." Mina wrinkled her nose. "And while you might miss seeing the ruffians, I don't mind a night out without them."

"They're a handful, then? Just like their father, yeah?"

She laughed. "Exactly like their father."

"Hey, man. Stop that," Kiah said, giving Zach one of those man-hugs that involved a lot of backslapping. "I'm under fire from all these women enough as it is. I can't wait for Benny-

Bop to get old enough to back up his old man. Right now, he's usually in the women's camp."

"As it should be," Mina retorted. "We're always right."

Gen laughed with them but couldn't ignore the little ache around her heart. Once upon a time she'd thought that by now she'd have a child of her own and a relationship as tight and loving as Kiah and Mina's.

Maybe it was time to accept that just wasn't in the cards for her, but accepting and being happy about it weren't the same thing.

The greeting Gen got from Kiah and Mina wasn't quite as warm, but she tried not to take it to heart. They didn't know that Zach wasn't in any danger of having his heart broken.

He didn't care enough about her for it to be a possibility.

After they'd all eaten, Gen volunteered to wash up, and Zach helped rinse, while Kiah dried. Mr. Lewin turned up the calypso music he'd been playing, and although no one danced, it really increased the fun atmosphere.

"Your mother is amazing," Kiah told Gen as he reached up to put away the plates. "A real live wire."

"That's one way to describe her," Gen laughed. "She really enjoys people and is genuinely curious about their lives, but some people think she's just plain nosy."

He laughed with her and gestured out the kitchen window toward the veranda with his chin. "Well, she might have met her match with Miss Pearl. By the end of the night they'll know all of each other's business. And Aunt Sheila's too, if she's not careful."

Gen and Zach moved to where Kiah was standing to see what he was pointing at, and there they were: Mrs. Lewin, Mom and Miss Pearl, sitting in a little group. As she watched, Gen saw Miss Pearl make a point, emphasized with a wave of both hands, and the two other ladies nodded. Then it was Mom who interjected, which was also followed by sage nods.

"Anyone else getting flashbacks of the *Macbeth* witches right now?" Zach asked, amusement evident in his voice. "I don't know whether to be happy they all seem to be getting along, or afraid."

"You two should be afraid," Kiah said in a dark tone. "Extremely afraid."

And although Gen laughed with them, she was intensely curious about the conversation going on outside.

Who knew what the heck Mom might be telling them about Gen and her life before St. Eustace?

She'd made the determined decision to leave her past behind, as much as possible, when she came to the island. Zach knew her better than anyone else here, and even he didn't know that much. Not the nitty-gritty, down and dirty, anyway.

And she preferred it that way. Then she didn't have to relive any of it or reveal the cowardly, dark corners of herself. The pieces she herself didn't realize existed until after the Bell's palsy and Johan's defection.

Mom knew most but not all of it; more than enough to expose parts of Gen she'd been jealously guarding. Gen didn't think she'd say anything untoward, but who knew?

Wiping her hands dry, she went and stood in the shadow of the doorway, feeling apart from the chatting, laughing group of people spread out before her. Manipulating her eyelid with the tip of her finger, she tried to gather the energy to put on a smile and rejoin the party.

When Zach's arms came around her waist and he placed his cheek against her head, she instinctively rested back against him, tension bleeding away in the presence of his warmth and strength.

"All right there, Gen?"

His breath tickled across her ear, making her shiver deliciously. What was it about this man that one touch immediately had her blood going to a low simmer of desire?

"Yes," she said, resisting the urge to tell him how much better she felt with his arms around her. "But I think Mom's trip is starting to catch up to her. I just saw her hiding a yawn."

"You're tired too." It wasn't a question, but a statement. "Time to get you home to bed."

The way he said it, his voice low and intimate, made her nipples peak and her legs tremble.

"I wish…"

She didn't have to elaborate. Zach's arms tightened, and he pressed a kiss to the spot just below her ear.

"Me too," he growled. Then he let her go, saying, "Go round up your mum, if you can pull her away."

But Mom was willing to concede to being ready to go.

"Hezekiah has a plan for us all to go to somewhere call Northern Cove tomorrow," she said, as she was taking her leave of everyone. "And I need to make sure I get enough rest."

It was a quiet drive to Gen's condo, a sure indication that Mom really was exhausted, since usually she'd be conducting a blow-by-blow review of the evening just gone.

And when Gen led her into the condo and then up to her room, Zach bringing up the rear with her bag, all she said was, "Oh, this is nice, dear."

Then she kissed them each good-night and shooed them out, firmly shutting the door behind them.

Gen and Zach exchanged looks, but he shook his head, then led her down the staircase and to the front door.

"I'm not making love to you with your mother in the room next door," he said, pulling her into his arms and resting his forehead on hers. "I've never made as much noise in bed in my life as I do with you. It's a little embarrassing."

She giggled, but said, "I know what you mean. I've never been a screamer either, but apparently you're turning me into one."

He sighed, his breath gusting across her face, and she inhaled, taking it into her lungs.

"I don't even think I can kiss you without wanting more," he said in the growly, gravelly tone she loved so much. "But I can't leave without kissing you either. It's a conundrum."

It wasn't for her, so she angled his face with her hand and placed her lips on his, initiating the kiss she was yearning for.

When they broke away several minutes later, Zach shook his head, and she couldn't interpret the expression in his eyes.

"You're addictive," was all he said, before dropping one more brief, hard, hot kiss on her lips.

Then he was gone, leaving her staring at the closed door and pressing her knuckle into the corner of her mouth.

"You are too," she whispered into the empty room.

CHAPTER THIRTEEN

THE NEXT COUPLE of days were a whirlwind of sightseeing, mostly directed by Mr. Lewin.

On the first day, they went to Northern Cove, which was about an hour and a half away. Setting off midmorning, they stopped to have lunch at a very nice restaurant in the hills, with a magnificent view over a valley with a river running through it.

The Cove itself was on a part of the island where the hills seemed to march right down into the sea, parting at the last moment to create a lovely sweep of beach. On the slopes above were dotted a series of large villas, many with steps carved straight into the rock, giving access to the beach.

"Years ago, some of the villa owners wanted to make this a private beach, but the public outcry put pay to the plan," Mr. Lewin said, settling under the umbrella, his slightly smug expression making Gen want to laugh.

"Are you coming into the water, Dad?" Mrs. Lewin asked him, as she took off her caftan, preparing to go into the sea.

But he shook his head. "Not yet. I just want to sit here and take in the scenery for a moment."

Gen saw the narrow-eyed glance Zach gave his father and, from professional habit, gave the older man a long, careful look.

Visually, she didn't see anything to give her concern, but she didn't know Mr. Lewin well enough to discern if he seemed unlike himself.

When they were in the water, she maneuvered Zach away from where their mothers were bobbing in the sea so they could talk without being overheard.

As though it was the most natural thing in the world, he pulled her into his arms, and she wrapped her legs around his waist so he held her aloft. Being so intimately close almost made her forget what she had planned to say, and she had to drag her brain away from wondering if anyone would notice if they made out.

"Is your dad feeling okay?" she asked, and his hands, which had been moving in slow circles along her skin, went still.

"I'm not sure," he replied, looking back to where his father was sitting, his face up to the sky, as though taking in the warmth of the sun. "I've caught him rubbing his chest a couple of times since he came, and usually he'd be in the water now or walking along the beach, but whenever I ask him if he's okay, he says he is."

They both watched the older man for a moment, and Gen said, "I think you might want to keep an eye on him, just in case."

As though aware of their scrutiny, Mr. Lewin suddenly got up and, taking off his shoes and shirt, strolled into the water to join his wife.

"There," Zach said, sounding relieved. "Maybe he did just want to soak in the scenery for a while. It's almost eight years since he's been back home."

Gen wasn't completely convinced but didn't want to belabor the point and make Zach anxious.

"That makes sense," she said, facing Zach and finding his gaze still, nevertheless, fixed on his father for a few moments more. "We should go back and join them. We're starting to drift farther away."

That brought his gaze back to hers, and the look in his eyes stole her breath.

"I know. That's by design. I just want you to myself for a few minutes."

"You're bad," she whispered through a suddenly tight throat, as his hand slipped beneath the elastic at the leg of her bikini bottoms.

"You make me that way," he said, his eyelids

getting slumberous, as he found her slick and ready for him. "I just want to make you come, just once. It's become my greatest pleasure, recently."

Glancing back, she realized their parents were now little more than dots in the distance. Reaching between them, she pushed the front of his trunks down.

"Two can play that game," she gasped, her breath already rushing and hitching as he expertly took her closer and closer to orgasm.

And they ended up getting out of the water far down the beach and walking slowly back so the blush of desire satisfied could fade from Gen's face before they got to the others.

The following day found them traveling even farther afield, visiting Lewin cousins who lived at the westernmost village on the island. They were expected, with the outing planned from when Mr. and Mrs. Lewin had arrived, but when Gen suggested that perhaps her mother and herself should forgo it, the idea was dismissed.

"I already told them you'd be coming," Mr. Lewin said. "And they were excited to meet you."

She sent Zach a wide-eyed look, but he just shrugged and shook his head slightly.

So they went, and Gen had to admit she had a wonderful time.

"Wear something cool, dear," Mrs. Lewin advised the night before. "It's hotter than the inside of the Devil's oven there."

And she was glad for the warning, which she also passed on to her mother.

The area was completely different from what she'd seen of the rest of the island, having an almost desert-like climate. And because so many people had been invited to see Hezekiah, Sheila and Zach, the party was held outside.

"It's like a crawfish boil," Mom said when she saw the huge pots over wood fires.

Of course, it wasn't crawfish in the pots, but the food was delicious nonetheless, and with the music blaring and children running back and forth, it was a wonderful hubbub.

They left at about four thirty, over the protests of their hosts, and wound their way back to Zach's house. There they sat on the veranda, some having tea, the others cool drinks, and discussing what to do for dinner, if they even wanted more food that day.

"I'm still stuffed," Mom said with a little groan. "I haven't seen that much food since last Mardi Gras."

Gen was about to agree when a movement down below caught her eye, and she turned to see a teenager furiously pedaling a bicycle along the road. Turning in through the gateposts at the end of the driveway, he vaulted off the bike and started running up toward the house.

Zach and Mr. Lewin were already on their feet, having also seen him.

"That's Collie," Zach said to his father. "Mass Alex's grandson."

"I thought so," came the reply. "Although last time I saw him, he was little more than a toddler."

The panting youth came to a halt as soon as he was within earshot, and called, "Missa Zach, Grandpa chop hisself with the 'lass, and we caan' stop the bleeding. Mama send mi come get you."

He spoke so quickly in the local dialect Gen couldn't follow what he was saying, but she was already on her feet, and as Zach hurried into the house, she followed.

"What—?"

"Mass Alex, our elderly neighbor, has cut himself with his machete and the bleeding won't stop. No, Dad," Zach told his father, who was following toward the steps. "Stay here. Gen and I will go, and if we need to take him to the hospital, we'll let you know."

On his way out, he detoured to grab a medical bag from his room, while Gen hurriedly got into his SUV. In no time at all they were rocketing down the driveway.

Collie had already jumped back on his bicycle and was out of sight when they turned onto the main track.

"Age of patient?" Gen asked, hanging on, as every dip in the road made the car bounce.

"In his eighties, at least. I don't know his medical history, but he told me once that besides some rheumatism, he was fine."

They flew past young Collie, and then Zach turned onto another narrower track, this one in much worse condition, but he didn't ease up on the gas, just swerved when he could to avoid the potholes.

Then, on the left, Gen saw an old wooden house and a little group of people standing in the yard, staring at the door.

Zach brought the vehicle to a screeching halt and was out before Gen even got her seat belt undone. She caught up to him as he grabbed the medical bag from the back seat and followed as he skirted the group and went up the rickety steps and into the house.

The old man was on the couch, two women bending over him, and Zach went straight to him.

The women gave him room, but Gen had to

say in the firm, authoritative voice she'd mastered, "Let me through. I'm a doctor."

One woman moved, but the other waited where she was, holding a bloody towel against the old man's leg.

"Mass Alex, what happened?" Zach asked, pulling out his blood pressure cuff while Gen took his pulse, which, thankfully, was still fairly strong.

"No so sure," Mass Alex said, his voice calm but quiet. "One minute, mi cutting grass, next mi on the ground, and the cutlass in mi leg. Troycus was with mi, and him pull it out and carry mi home."

"Pulse two-plus," she told Zach, after he'd finished the BP reading.

"Eighty over fifty," he replied.

"Is that the pretty doctor lady your daddy tell mi 'bout the other day?"

Mass Alex smiled at her, but Gen gave him a stern look as she pulled on a pair of gloves.

"None of that flirting right now, sir," she said, even though she winked as she checked his dorsalis pedis and then the posterior tibial pulses. "Dorsalis fair. Posterior tibial weak," she reported to Zach.

He nodded, looking grim. "Mass Alex, Dr. Broussard is going to look at your leg, and it might hurt, okay?"

Mass Alex nodded and closed his eyes.

The woman holding the towel moved aside then, ceding the position to Gen.

When she lifted it, she realized the severity of the wound.

"Laceration approximately seven centimeters in length, into the lateral gastrocnemius muscle. Free-flowing bleeding makes it impossible to see how deep it is." Putting the towel back in place and applying pressure, she asked the patient, "Sir, are you on any anticoagulants?"

"What's that?" the old man asked, opening his eyes.

"Are you on any medications to stop your blood from clotting?"

"He's not on any medication at all," the younger of the two women in the room said. "Grandpa's always been real healthy."

Zach was pulling gauze out of his kit, and Gen asked, "Do you have a pressure cuff in there?"

He handed her the gauze and cuff, then shifted down to assist her.

"I'm not going to try to wrap it," she told him. "Manipulating the leg too much will induce further bleeding. We'll pad it with the gauze and lift it just far enough to slide the cuff into place. I take it calling an ambulance is out of the question?"

"Quicker to drive him to the hospital than to try to explain where we are," he replied as she prepared a thick gauze pad.

"We're going to have to figure out why he's bleeding so profusely when we get him to the hospital." Looking at the young woman who'd been holding the towel in place, Gen continued, "Please hold his heel, and when I tell you, lift his foot up, but just a few inches, okay?"

Just the act of removing the towel to place the pad and inflate the cuff brought another gush of blood. But Gen was relatively sure the even, constant pressure on the wound should be enough to get him to the hospital without Mass Alex going into hypovolemic shock.

"Can you put down the back seat so we have more room to lay him down and elevate his leg?"

"Yes."

When he went out to get the vehicle ready, Gen stripped off her gloves and scooted closer to Mass Alex's head.

"How are you feeling?" she asked, touching his face and finding it worryingly cool to the touch.

But the old man grinned, revealing an expanse of gum, within which resided three lonely teeth.

"Better for looking at you instead of that ugly man."

Gen could only laugh softly and shake her head at his nonsense.

"Papa, yuh behave yuhself," the older of the two women said, but her scolding couldn't disguise the worry in her voice.

Gen looked up at her. "Has your father had any issues lately, with bleeding or bruising easily?"

The two women exchanged a glance, and then Mass Alex's daughter replied, "Yes, now I think on it. Every minute I see a scrape on him, and sometimes all three-four days before any little cut him get stop bleed."

There was some banging and shouting from outside, then Zach came in with two other men, one of whom was carrying a narrow door.

"Good idea," Gen said. "And I think a cervical collar for safety, since we don't know what additional damage might have been done when he fell."

They quickly fitted the collar and, with the help of the two other men, Zach and Mass Alex's granddaughter, they eased him from the couch onto the door.

"I need something to elevate his leg," Gen told his daughter, who had tears in her eyes, as she watched her father being carried outside. "Can I take the cushions off the couch?"

"Anything you need," she said, her voice hitching. "Take anything."

Gen took a quick moment to squeeze the woman's arm. "We're going to do the best we can for him, okay?"

The woman nodded. "I called my son, and he's coming here, so I'll get him to carry me to the hospital."

"Good," Gen said, heading for the door when she heard Zach toot the horn. "See you there."

She arranged the cushions on either side of the old man to keep him from sliding around too much and, with Zach's help, elevated his leg on the last cushion. After covering him with an emergency blanket from the medical kit, she sat in the back with him, and Zach put the vehicle, which he'd already turned around, into gear. As they carefully navigated down the hill, Gen kept tabs on the patient's vitals, but she was worried about the clamminess of his skin and the way he seemed to be drifting in and out of consciousness.

As soon as they turned onto the main road, she said, "As fast as you safely can, Zach."

And he put his foot down. Using the hands-free capabilities in the vehicle, he called ahead to the hospital and told them who they were bringing in, and what had happened. Kiah came on the line.

"I'm on duty, and I'll meet you in emerge."

They were still at least ten minutes out when, all of a sudden, a police vehicle pulled out in front of them from a side road and turned on its siren. Zach slowed slightly, but an arm came out of the window, beckoning him to follow, and with their unexpected escort, they made it to the hospital in half the time.

Gen clambered out of the vehicle as soon as Zach opened the back. Orderlies were on hand to lift Mass Alex out and onto a stretcher, and she took that time to update Kiah on her findings and suspicions.

Then the stretcher was being rushed into the hospital, leaving Zach and her outside the door, watching as the team on duty took over.

Zach looked dazed, a little lost, and Gen put her hand on his arm.

"He means a lot to you, doesn't he?"

He nodded, swallowed. "In a strange way, I feel as though he's the last link to my grandad. He's always telling me stories about the family, and how things were even before I was born."

"I think he'll be okay," she said gently, wanting to hold him, but sensing a sudden distance between them she neither understood nor knew how to breach. "They just need to figure out why he isn't clotting the way he should. And he's in great hands with Kiah."

Zach straightened his back and nodded. "You're right. Let's head back up to the house. His daughter should be here soon."

It didn't feel right—as in, what would be right for Zach in this moment. He was sad and worried, and she understood he didn't want her comfort, but he needed something to make him feel better.

"Wait," she said to his already retreating back, and he paused, almost at his car door, to look back at her. "I need to clean up," she said, gesturing to her blood-stained blouse. "And change. Why don't you stay with Mass Alex until his daughter comes while I run home?"

He gave her one of those unfathomable looks, and she knew he'd completely shut her out when he nodded and said, "Good idea. Just call me when you're coming back, yeah?"

And then he walked into the hospital without a backward glance.

CHAPTER FOURTEEN

ZACH GOT PERMISSION to stay in the room with Mass Alex while Kiah ran tests, but got kicked out soon after. Which, after he'd called to update his father, left him sitting in the waiting room with too much time to think.

Just four more days, he reminded himself, and he could try to get on with his life without this sensation of drowning each time he looked at Gen.

Glancing back in the rearview mirror, seeing the tenderness in her profile as she comforted Mass Alex had his heart turning over and made him realize just how deep in he already was.

She was everything a man could ever hope for, but she wasn't for him, and they both knew it. No matter how explosive they were in bed or how much he admired and was attracted to her, this was just a dream. A fantasy not destined to last.

Perhaps, for her it was purely a matter of enjoyment, but if the last few days had shown him anything, it was just how dangerous she was to his heart.

Now all he had to do was convince himself that once her mother was gone, things could and would go back to normal. That they'd maybe stay friends and be good work colleagues, but this interminable desire he had for her would fade.

After all, he'd been with Moira for more than a decade, had been convinced he'd always love her. Now he realized she'd hardly crossed his mind in the last few weeks. And when she had, it was as a cautionary reminder, rather than the memory reactivating the heartbreak and hurt of before.

Realizing he'd got over Moira was a relief, but it didn't mean he was ready to put his heart on the line again anytime soon, and especially not with Gen. Things were going well while they put on this show for her mum, but he knew he'd never hold her interest for long.

Earlier in the day, her mother had taken his arm and asked him to walk with her down to the salt flat near his cousin's house.

As they stood looking at the shimmering mirages caused by the sun on the surface, she'd said, "Zachary, I know ViVi seems so open and easy to know, but beneath that persona is a complex woman, who's gone through a great deal of hardship and pain. More, I think, than even she acknowledges. It's changed her, and not always in positive ways."

He'd waited, hoping she'd elaborate, but instead she'd patted his arm, and said, "Remember that, please, if anything happens. Now, let's go back before she thinks I'm telling you secrets."

What else could that have been but a warning not to assume things were as they seemed, and that he shouldn't be hurt when things went wrong?

And of course, her mother didn't even know the truth about how their "relationship" came into being.

If you added that in, it spelled disaster for him, should he lose sight of reality.

Leaning forward, he put his elbows on his knees and rubbed his hands over the top of his head, suddenly tired—exhausted from his grinding thoughts.

Why couldn't he be like Gen—seemingly carefree despite the past and able to just have some fun? The consummate actress, making everyone around her believe her performance without losing herself completely in it.

Even he, if he weren't careful, would get sucked in by it and forget it was all playacting.

He wished he knew whether they were in the midst of a farce, a drama or a comedy of errors.

"Hi, man." Kiah's voice brought him out of his reverie. "We're taking Mass Alex into surgery in a little while, and from what I've seen, I'm thinking perhaps vitamin K deficiency as the source of the bleeding, although I'm running further tests to see what's causing it. If it's malabsorption syndrome, then we have to figure out which organ is responsible."

"But you think he'll be okay?"

Kiah's lips twisted to the side briefly. "I believe so, cuz, but you have to remember his age and how difficult rehabilitation may be for him after surgery. Unfortunately, anything is possible, but you know we're doing the best we can for him."

"Yeah, I know it," he replied, looking up to see Doritt, Mass Alex's daughter, followed by what seemed like the entire family. "Here come his relatives."

Just as he was making sure Doritt knew Kiah, and explaining her grandfather was under his care, his phone rang. Excusing himself, he walked away to answer, feeling stupid because his heart missed a beat when he saw Gen's name on the screen.

"Hi, are you ready to go, or do you need more time?"

Taking a deep breath, he strove for normalcy, although he still felt jittery and sad and annoyed, all at once.

"I'm ready. Doritt, Mass Alex's daughter, is here now, and he's about to go into surgery to repair the muscle. Kiah will call when it's over and let us know how it went."

"Okay. Shall I pick you up down by emerge?"

"Yes, please."

"I'm on my way."

Outside, the bustle of the town could be heard in the distance; the honking of horns, the booming bass line of a Saturday night dance. Closer at hand were the sounds of the hospital; chatter and the *clang* of a gate swinging closed. The rattle of a gurney.

All familiar now, but nothing in comparison to London, where the throngs of people, the constant hum of traffic and the bright lights used to exhilarate his soul. There, you could get every conceivable type of cuisine, buy any product, find any kind of entertainment as long as you knew where to look.

Once upon a time, he'd lived for the days when he'd be home from active duty and could experience it all, gorging himself on the hurry and uproar of the city.

Now, as though in response to the mental and emotional upheaval he was experiencing, he realized he no longer craved all those things. He'd found peace, and satisfaction, on St. Eustace, and he might never go back to England to live.

Funny how, when you find yourself at a crossroad in life and think you know where you are, sometimes you're facing in a completely different direction than you imagined.

When he came here, it was with the idea of having a quiet place to lick his wounds and the opportunity to help Dad out by getting the house repaired. He'd never entertained the thought of staying permanently, and he wasn't quite sure why he was contemplating it now. Yet, it felt right.

And it made his decision to try to keep his head on straight when it came to Gen even more important. She was a big-city girl, here just for a while. Not only could he not hold her interest, but he suspected St. Eustace wouldn't either.

Even her mother seemed to think the same and was anticipating having her daughter back in New Orleans.

"Hey you." Gen's voice startled him, and he was surprised to realize she'd driven up and he hadn't even noticed. "What're you doing?"

He saw her reach for the seat belt, and said, "I was just woolgathering. Do you mind driving up?"

"Sure," she said, snapping the buckle back into place. "Jump in."

As they drove along he tried to ignore the sweet vanilla scent emanating from Gen's side of the car, even though it filled his head and made his body tighten. To keep his mind off it, he relayed all the information Kiah had given him and heard her sigh.

"I hope he makes it through okay. He's a sweet old man, and I know how much he means to you."

When she swung into a small strip mall, he asked, "Why are we stopping here?"

"I ordered some Chinese food, just in case anyone's hungry. If not, we can have it as leftovers tomorrow."

As she said it, his stomach grumbled loudly.

Gen paused, half in, half out of the vehicle, and looked back at him.

"Good idea, I guess?"

And the amusement on her face chased the last of his worries to the back of his mind as they shared yet another laugh together.

Zach was still a little withdrawn when she picked him up at the hospital, but since he seemed to snap out of it, she put it down to worry about Mass Alex.

Different people dealt with stress in different ways, and maybe withdrawing was his?

She also had to remind herself that theirs wasn't the type of relationship where they shared their deepest secrets or expressed emotions to each other.

Which was just as well, really, since she didn't want to get to the point where she was so comfortable with him—or anyone else—that she left herself vulnerable. She knew all too well where that could lead and had no interest in that kind of pain.

Once in a lifetime was more than enough.

At the house, as she parked, Zach said, "Thanks for driving. I just didn't feel up to it."

As the dome light came on, she could see lines bracketing his mouth and the tired set to his eyes, and she replied, "I'll call a taxi to take Mom and me home."

He shook his head, reaching for the door handle. "I'll be okay once I have a chance to relax for a little. I had a bit of an adrenaline dump at the hospital."

"Understandable."

They met up at the path, and Puss let out a *murp* at them as they passed by on the way to the door, but didn't get up.

"Is it my imagination, or is that cat getting lazier by the day?" she asked.

As if in response, Puss yawned, and Zach chuckled as he gave the cat a little tickle under her chin.

"I think you got your answer right there."

Mrs. Lewin met them at the top of the stairs.

"Dad was that worried about Mass Alex, I'm afraid he's got into the rum."

Mother and son exchanged a glance, and then Gen saw Mrs. Lewin's gaze slide her way for an instant before she continued, "Marielle's entertaining him, but I'm not sure..."

There it was again, Gen thought, that unfathomable expression on Zach's face she'd yet to learn how to interpret.

He shrugged and bent to kiss his mom's cheek.

"It'll be okay, Mum. Gen's pretty much family now, aren't you, love?"

Then he strolled off, carrying the bag of food, leaving both women staring at his back.

Shaking her head, wondering what he was up to, Gen turned to Mrs. Lewin and said, "If you prefer we leave—"

"I'll take you home after I've eaten," Zach interjected. "And, in case you're worried, Dad's not a violent drunk. He just gets maudlin and talks too much."

"Oh," Gen said weakly, not sure what else *to* say.

Mrs. Lewin pursed her lips, her gaze going from her son to the door leading outside, then back again. She sighed and shook her head.

"If you say so, Zachary. But he'll be working himself up to singing *Danny Boy* soon."

Zach grunted, taking down a plate. "Won't that be a treat."

A little annoyed at him for the way he'd dismissed his mom's concerns, although knowing he'd had a hard evening, Gen turned her back on him and gave his mother one of her best smiles.

"Well, if he needs a companion who also talks too much, he couldn't have found a better one in Mom."

That, at least, made Zach's mother smile.

Outside, though, Gen realized why Sheila had been worried. Her husband was in full spate, sounding as though he was already beyond worked up.

"We're simple, hardworking folk, but some don't think much of us—me a bus driver, Sheila looking after old folk. But our daughter has two degrees—two—and works for the foreign office. And Zach, he would have been a doctor, like your girl, if he hadn't got caught up with—"

"That's enough now, Dad." Sheila's voice cracked like a whip, making everyone, even Mr. Lewin, jump, and leaving Gen wondering what, exactly, he had been about to say. "I'm sure Marielle doesn't give a fig for any of your nonsense, and Zach wouldn't thank you for talking about his private business."

"No, I wouldn't." Zach came out with a plate in his hand. "There's some Chinese takeout inside, if anyone wants some."

His tone seemed aimed at putting an end to the entire conversation, but Gen couldn't leave it there. Not when it was clear Mr. Lewin didn't appreciate his son's accomplishments.

"For the record," she said quietly, keeping her gaze fixed on Mr. Lewin's, "Zach's not only one of the finest nurses I've ever worked with, if not the best, but I'm here to tell you that in an emergency, I'd want a nurse to help me, over most of the doctors I know."

"Leave it, Gen," Zach said. "He doesn't care."

"He *should* care." Frustrated, Gen waved her hands for emphasis. "Nurses like Zach are… are…" She searched for an appropriate analogy and came up with, "They're like Ginger Rogers. She did everything Fred Astaire did, but she had to do it backward and in high heels. The doctors get the glory, but it's the nurses that really keep everything together and running smoothly."

"No, no, I proud of him." Mr. Lewin's South London accent suddenly seemed to fall away, replaced with the St. Eustace vernacular of his youth. "But we work so hard, him Mum and me, to make sure him have a better life…"

"That's what we all want, isn't it?" Mom said, as Mr. Lewin's voice faltered. "What we all try so desperately to achieve. Making sure our children do better than their parents. My grandmother had that same dream. She was born in the backwoods of Louisiana, and she moved to New Orleans and became a maid. Years later, my mother, bless her, used to try to fancy it up and tell her church friends Nanoni had been a housekeeper.

"And Nanoni would say, 'Ah weren't no housekeeper, Delphina. Your mama was a *maid*.' But through her hard work my mom got to go to school and became a teacher."

Gen smiled at hearing her mother so faithfully re-create her great-grandmother's drawl, which she remembered from her early childhood. When she glanced at Zach, his gaze was fixed on her face, and heat trickled down her spine.

Then he looked back at his plate, and the connection was lost.

"I'm proud of my son," Mrs. Lewin said, in an almost defiant tone. "I'm proud of all my children."

"I am of mine too," Mom said, sending a little smile Gen's way. "None homeless or in jail, all gainfully employed. What more can a mother ask?"

That made them all laugh, although the fraught conversation still hung between them, like smoke.

"Just one more," Mr. Lewin said, trying to lever himself out of the low chair he was in and failing. Slumping back, he waved his glass and said, "Son, fix your old man a rum, nuh?"

"Oh, no, you don't," Mrs. Lewin said, getting up and plucking the tumbler out of his hand. "It's bedtime for you."

"Need a hand, Mum?"

"If you don't mind, on the steps."

With Mrs. Lewin on one side and Zach on the other, Mr. Lewin departed for the evening. And Gen and her mother exchanged a laughing look when a strained, falsetto rendition of *Danny Boy* came wavering up the staircase.

"I wonder what Mr. Lewin was about to say?" she mused aloud. "About what stopped Zach becoming a doctor."

"Does it matter, ViVi? Whatever decisions Zachary made back then can't be changed, can they?"

"No, but—"

"Either you accept him as he is, or you don't. It's really that simple."

Her curiosity had nothing to do with accepting him, since she thought he was amazing just the way he was. Rather, she wanted to know everything of importance about him, to understand him better.

But before she could say so, the man in question stepped out onto the veranda and said, "Let me take you ladies home before it gets any later."

It was a quiet trip back down to Gen's condo, and, once there, Zach walked them to the front door but made no effort to come inside.

"Are we still on for the botanical gardens tomorrow?" she asked after he'd said good-night, and was turning to go.

He glanced back and shrugged. "I'll let you know in the morning. I have a feeling Dad might want to go visit Mass Alex in the hospital."

"Okay," she said, wondering at his coolness and the lack of even a kiss on the cheek. He'd resumed his walk to the car, when, unable to leave it alone, she called, "Zach, is everything all right?"

He stopped and turned to face her, bland expression firmly in place.

"Yeah. Why wouldn't it be?"

Then, not waiting for a reply, he lifted a hand in farewell and left.

CHAPTER FIFTEEN

THE NEXT MORNING Zach awoke at the usual time, but lay in bed for a few minutes, trying to shake the mood he'd gone to bed with and that still lingered like a sore tooth.

Last evening had been an exhausting debacle. As if poor Mass Alex's injury and Dad's tirade weren't enough, hearing Marielle Broussard tell Gen she either had to accept him as he was, or not at all, had felt like the last straw.

He hadn't heard the first part of the conversation, but he'd heard enough to be angry.

Gen really was the consummate actress, wasn't she? Defending him to his father in a way that made Zach feel like a giant, even while secretly disdainful enough that her mother noticed and took her to task.

The simmering anger he felt was, he knew, ridiculous under the circumstances.

She had the absolute right to view him however she pleased, especially since it was all a big hoax anyway. For all he knew, Gen was setting the scene for their eventual "breakup."

But no matter what her motivations, it still rankled.

He could have sworn she wasn't the two-faced type, and everything he'd thought he knew about her made her speech to his father ring completely true. Yet, he'd be the first to admit his track record on accurately judging character was poor.

There was no use lying around, thinking about a situation he had very little control over, so he threw off the covers and sat on the edge of the bed.

What he could control, though, was how much further he allowed the physical side of the relationship with Gen to go. As fantastically amazing as making love with her was, it would be best, especially for him, if they didn't do that anymore. He had come to realize he couldn't easily separate physical attraction from emotional, and each time he was intimate with Gen drew him closer to falling for her.

He chuckled grimly, acknowledging he was already there. If he weren't already emotionally involved, none of this would matter, yeah? She could say whatever she wanted, think whatever she wanted of him, and it wouldn't hurt. But, just as it still hurt to hear Dad express disappointment at his career path, knowing Gen, too, thought less of him because of his job was definitely painful.

Both hurt because of the people involved.

Enough.

Pushing off the bed, he quickly dressed, the restlessness of spirit driving him to do something other than go into the garden. While he often found solace in the quietude of mornings among the plants, today he needed more physical activity to help get his whirling brain calmed down.

His parents weren't up yet, so he left a note on the kitchen counter and went for a run through the fields near the house.

It was the perfect blend of flat and undulating topography, which allowed him to vary his pace and forced him to think about how he expended his energy. Normally he ran for about an hour, but this morning he let the meditative rhythm of his strides carry him farther than usual before turning for home.

About a hundred meters from the driveway, he slowed to a jog and then used the walk up to the house as his cool-down exercise.

To his surprise, he could see his mother and Mrs. Broussard on the veranda, and when he got to the back of the house, Gen was sitting under the gazebo, a cup of coffee in hand. She was wearing shorts, exposing her long, toned legs, and an off the shoulder top in a peachy color that made her skin luminous. Just the sight of her had his heart rate going back up and his fingertips tingling with the urge to touch, and he silently cursed himself for reacting that way.

Drawing closer, he realized she was wearing what he thought of as her beauty queen smile, used as either shield to hide behind or weapon for fending others off.

Impossible to know which one it signified this morning.

"You're here early," he remarked, as he headed to the tank to get the hose, needing something to do with his hands. Something to focus on, other than the beautiful, infuriating woman still smiling so broadly at him.

"Your mom called to ask if I'd heard from you since she couldn't find you and was getting worried."

"I left her a note." Untangling the hose, he turned on the spigot. Adjusting the stream of water, he began misting the plants, watching as the droplets formed rainbows in the sunlight.

"Yes. It had blown off the counter. I found it under the table when I got here."

"Well, sorry for her bothering you so early." He knew he sounded churlish, but it was in an attempt at self-preservation. There was something about Gen that was impossible to resist, but he'd do his damnedest to keep his distance—both physically and emotionally.

"I didn't mind," Gen said. "We were already up, and I got worried too. It wasn't like you to just disappear like that, without telling someone where you were going."

Both her false solicitousness and assumption that she somehow knew him, after so short a time and considering their faux relationship, made his temper start to simmer. Reining in the words on the tip of his tongue, he gave a noncommittal grunt instead.

"I called the hospital," she continued. "Since Mass Alex had a bad night, they're limiting visitors to family, but so far the prognosis is still good."

"Okay, so we're on for the gardens?"

"According to your father, yes, we are."

"Right. I'll finish up here and go shower, then we can head out."

He was trying to take a leaf out of her book—be calm, and smile—but it wasn't easy. Then it became more difficult when she got up and stood next to him.

Immediately, her scent surrounded him, filling his head, reminding him of how it felt to hold her, touch her, give her pleasure and receive ecstasy in return.

"Zach, are you still annoyed about what your father said last night?"

His first impulse was to pretend he didn't know what she was talking about, but while that type of deflection might work with some people, he knew it wouldn't work with Gen.

He shrugged. Even got the corners of his lips to curl upward, as though amused by the whole thing. "Dad didn't say anything last night I haven't heard a hundred times before."

"Doesn't mean it doesn't hurt to hear it again."

If he didn't know better, he'd swear the compassion in her voice was real, but he knew better. He'd known better from the beginning, but had lost sight of reality when he took her in his arms and gave in to the attraction.

He walked away from her, striving for control, hoping she'd let the whole thing drop.

"It all happened a long time ago, and I'm over his disappointment, even if he isn't. So, don't worry about it."

Glancing back, he saw her pressing her knuckle into the corner of her mouth, but she had on dark glasses, so he couldn't gauge her thoughts.

Strange to realize he'd come to depend on her eyes to tell him things her facial expressions wouldn't.

He'd turned off the water and started rolling

up the hose when she said, "What really stopped you from becoming a doctor, Zach? And don't tell me it was the finances or you were bored. I'm not stupid. I know there's more to it than that. What did you get mixed up in that changed your plans?"

Taking a deep breath, he tried to rein in his knee-jerk reaction to her soft words, biting his tongue to stop himself from saying things he shouldn't.

Hanging the hose back on its hook, he told himself to let it go. Let it pass. But now it was her hypocrisy that made his blood boil, and he couldn't resist walking back to stand right in front of her, getting up close and personal.

They were almost nose to nose when he said quietly, "You made the rules about this fake relationship, and they didn't include me blabbing my business to you, yeah? You don't need to know every little thing about me to fool your mother into believing you're doing all right, so don't expect to get more than you're willing to give."

Her breath hitched, and her lips parted, but no words came out.

Zach nodded. "Right. I'm not stupid either, Gen. We both have pasts we don't want to talk about, so don't push me to tell you mine, es-

pecially when you have no interest in recipro-
cating."

Then, because those gorgeous lips were right
there, and he was far thirstier for them than he
should, he kissed her, hard.

But if he'd set out to punish or make a point,
by the time her arms went around his waist, and
his hands were cradling the back of her head,
he knew the only one in purgatory was him.

And if he could stay there forever, he would.

Finally, he pulled back, trying to get his
breathing under control, glad to hear the air
rushing in and out of her lungs too.

"I'm going to shower."

Despite his best efforts, the words came out
as a rasp, and it took every ounce of willpower
to let her go and walk away.

As Gen watched Zach walk toward the house,
she pressed trembling fingers to her lips and
had to admit he was right.

This whole mess was her idea and she'd made
the rules. Even when the physical aspect of their
relationship changed, they'd agreed not to get
emotionally involved.

At least, *he'd* made it clear that it would be
unwise for her to get emotionally involved. Now
that she had, she had only herself to blame.

But most importantly, what he'd said about

her holding back, not being willing to talk about her own past, hit her like a blow to the solar plexus.

No, she didn't want to tell him about her past; about the dark place she'd gone to, revealing her weaknesses and fears.

Opening herself up to the pity she'd faced before.

Yet, she'd expected him to let her into *his* past life. Hoped that somehow, someway, there might be an opportunity to build on the mutual attraction and make what was fake, real.

But do it without revealing her own vulnerabilities and shame.

Shaking her head at her own temerity, she picked up her coffee mug and made her way inside, stopping to scratch the top of Puss's head just outside the door. Since Zach had started feeding the cat, she'd put on a little weight and become friendlier, but it was clear her feline heart belonged to Zach.

"Don't blame you, at all," she told the cat, who narrowed her eyes in seeming superiority. "He is rather irresistible, isn't he?"

Upstairs, Mom was sitting out on the veranda, sipping her coffee and looking out on the view. Mr. and Mrs. Lewin, she said, were getting ready for their day out.

"Although poor Hezekiah does look a little the worse for wear," she whispered with a smile.

Gen dug up an answering smile, but she knew she hadn't fooled her mother with the effort when Mom reached over and patted her hand.

Shaking her head in response, glad she had on her glasses so the moisture in her eyes wasn't visible, she leaned back in her chair, brain whirring.

It was easy to admit to herself how much she cared about Zach, and even how she craved him physically. Equally simple to entertain the thought of their relationship becoming a true one—but to what end, when she wasn't willing to reveal all the parts of herself that were unlovely and unlovable?

If her past experiences had taught her anything, it was the necessity of being honest, no matter what the relationship. Yet, here she was, caught up in a huge lie just to appease her mother, rather than standing up for herself and speaking her truth.

Before getting to know Zach, she hadn't wanted a relationship, not even a casual one. How do you dare trust again when two of the people you had utmost faith in betrayed you, publicly, and at the time when you needed them most?

When the experience left you feeling as

though you'd entered some alternate reality, because nothing felt safe or solid or even recognizably normal. Not for a long, long time, with the aftereffects of the cataclysmic shift echoing for months and years afterward.

Oh, she'd acted as though she'd gotten over it, once past the initial seismic shock and attendant reactions, but instead she'd pushed it all down, deep inside, where it festered. Her ability to discern truth from fiction, her worth, her value as a woman, a lover or a friend were all now uncertain.

Work, her talent and medical ability, became her one solace.

Here was something she controlled, and no one but her could cause to be called into question. Yet that focus on work to the exclusion of most everything else caused its own problems, and the overload to her system had taken her within inches of burnout.

St. Eustace had given her a place to decompress and start over, but through her own machinations, she was endangering the peace and happiness she'd found.

If she were going to make it right, she needed to come clean, starting with her mother.

And there was no time like the present.

"Mom, there's something I need to tell you—"

"We're ready to go." Mrs. Lewin stepped out

onto the veranda, her bag in one hand, a sun hat in the other. "Zach and Hezekiah are already down at the car."

As they rose, Mom said, "Can it wait until later, ViVi?"

"Sure. There's no rush."

There was even that cowardly part of herself that, dreading the fallout, hoped the conversation could be put off forever.

CHAPTER SIXTEEN

THE ST. EUSTACE BOTANICAL GARDENS were only about fifteen minutes outside of Port Michael, but on the opposite side of the town from the Lewins' home. Located on a twenty-acre site, it consisted of a large grassy area with multiple flower beds and a bandstand, surrounded by terraced fields and trees going up the hillsides on three sides. Walking paths wound through the various sectors, which were dotted with sculptures and plaques describing the history and provenance of the plants and artwork.

It was a perfect day to visit—hot, yes, because it was summer after all, but with a lovely breeze blowing up from the sea, which made it bearable.

After the excitement of the day before, Gen thought it would be nice to have a leisurely stroll through the lush grounds, except her unsettled spirit refused to allow her any peace.

In her all-or-nothing style, she'd wanted to

get her talk with her mother over with as soon as possible, but fate, or karma, or whatever was afoot didn't give her a chance. All the parents, seemingly in some kind of pact, stuck together like glue.

Mr. Lewin was in his element.

"One of my uncles was a sculptor, and some of his work is on display here," he said, casting a narrow-eyed gaze around the gardens. "One near the bandstand and others up higher, toward the lookout platform at the top of the terraces."

They were strolling through the lower gardens, where the beds were a mass of vivid color, the summer flowers blooming in all their glory.

"It's a shame there are so few people here," Mr. Lewin said, as they made their way toward the bandstand to look for the promised statue. "It used to be crowded on a weekend."

"Well, it is summer, Dad," Zach said. "Most people are at the beach, yeah?"

"It was different in my day," his father replied. "Saturday we could gallivant, as your grandmother called it, which included going to the beach or even a picture show if you'd made a little money that week doing work on the farm. But Sunday—now, that was for church, a big lunch and then coming to the gardens to hear a band play."

"I find we don't have family traditions anymore, the way we used to," Mom said. "Or, more importantly, rites of passage, leading us from one stage in life to another."

"It's hard to maintain a lot of those rituals now," Mrs. Lewin agreed. "There are too many distractions."

And as the older folks commiserated with each other about the decline of civilization, Gen and Zach exchanged a laughing glance, the first one for the day. It raised her spirits and sent a familiar tingle of awareness along her spine.

Then he looked away, and the connection was broken, leaving her bereft.

The statue was a minimalist depiction of the indigenous Kalinago people, who had inhabited the island long before Europeans even knew it existed.

"Our family has Kalinago blood," Mr. Lewin told them. "And my uncle was fascinated by their culture and place in St. Eustace's past. He led an initiative to include Kalinago history in the school curriculums. That was your gran's brother," he added, speaking to Zach. "He died when I was a young man, though, so you never had a chance to meet him."

"You should write all this down, Dad," Zach said. "So we can pass the information on and it doesn't get lost.

Mr. Lewin laughed and shook his head. "I'm

no scholar. Just thinking about writing sixty-odd years of stories down makes my head hurt. Let's go up toward the lookout, see if we can find Uncle Erwin's other pieces."

Behind the bandstand was a sloping ramp leading to the interconnected pathways, and they all went that way, Zach and Gen falling behind their parents. As they walked, Zach slung his arm around her shoulder, and Gen cursed herself for the way her awareness of him was dramatically heightened by his closeness.

He'd been cool and distant since their run-in that morning, but although in her head she was thinking she should maintain some emotional distance, it made no difference to her body. It reacted in a way that told her, no matter how things ended up between them, these weeks of being with him would be indelibly imprinted on her brain.

And heart.

Should she tell him she was going to confess to her mom first, or wait until after she had?

It was hard to make a decision when her brain kept short-circuiting because his scent filled her head and their bodies moved in perfect synchronicity as they walked. It reminded her of other times they'd moved as one.

Intimate times.

Yet, even with him right beside her, the chasm

that had opened between them over the last two days felt wider than ever. In the past they would have been talking and laughing together, but what had started out as a caper had turned serious so quickly, she was at a loss as to how to handle it.

Feigning interest in a mermaid statue, she paused, letting the parents go farther ahead, knowing in her heart what she needed to do.

She already knew the only way to make any of this right was with honesty, but while she'd thought to start with her mom, she should really begin with coming clean to Zach.

She touched Zach's wrist, where it lay over her shoulder. "You don't have to pretend to be into me anymore, if you don't want to. As soon as I get a chance, I plan to confess to Mom what I did, so you'll be off the hook."

He stiffened, his arm going rigid. Then, before she knew what he was planning to do, they were off the main path, with him steering her into a small thicket of trees. Deeper in, until they were hidden from sight of the trail.

When he turned her to face him, his lips were tight, and anger came off him in almost visible waves.

"You're a right little madam, aren't you? Just wanting to do whatever you want without a thought for anyone else."

Shocked, she stared at him, trying to figure out what he meant. "Why are you so angry? I thought you'd be pleased to end this farce."

The sound he made was feral. A guttural negation of her words.

Before she could say anything more, he was kissing her, his lips fierce. Punishing at first, then, as desire spiked and she kissed him back just as ferociously, it devolved into a passionate frenzy of lips and tongues.

His hands swept the elastic neckline of her top down, and his thumb dipped beneath her bra, sweeping over her nipple, tightening it to an aching peak. He bent his leg, bringing one thigh up between hers, and Gen bit back a moan of need at the contact.

"Does this feel like a farce?" he demanded as he bent to suck her nipple into the damp, erotic heat of his mouth.

She couldn't answer, too lost in the moment and the sensations firing along her nerve endings.

Who knew how far they would have gone if they hadn't heard hurrying footsteps on the main trail and her mom calling their names?

Zach straightened, and although she couldn't see his eyes because of his dark glasses, she could feel his gaze boring into hers.

"We'll finish this later," he growled as she

tidied her clothes with shaking hands. "We're here," he replied, as Mom called out for them again.

"Hurry," she said. "Your father's unwell."

Zach froze for a moment, and then they were running back through the trees to the path and in the direction her mother was pointing, everything else but Mr. Lewin's well-being forgotten.

As they rounded the next corner on the trail, Zach saw his dad sitting on a bench, Mum beside him, trying to get him to put his head between his knees.

"Stop," Dad said, batting her hand away. "That hurts."

Zach had left Gen in his dust and skidded to a halt to drop to one knee beside his father. "What's going on, Dad? Where hurts?"

He automatically took his father's wrist between his fingers, habit taking over, as Dad replied, "Nothing for you lot to be going on about. Just felt a little light-headed for a second."

"He almost fainted," Mum said, her voice wavering. "Looked set to topple right over."

"Nonsense." But Zach heard the breathless nature of his father's voice. "Just a bit of a turn."

Gen was there, and she began examining him, peppering him and Mum with questions about Dad's medications, whether he'd taken them that morning and what other symptoms he'd been experiencing.

Dad seemed disinclined to cooperate, actually sounding rather surly as he kept reiterating there was nothing wrong. Zach was about to take him to task when Gen beat him to it.

Putting her hand on his father's shoulder and looking him directly in the face, she said, "Your heart rate is elevated. You're short of breath, and your skin is clammy. Over the last couple of days, I've seen you periodically rub your chest as though suffering discomfort. Whether you will admit it or not, there's something going on, and we need to figure out what it is."

Dad just stared, apparently gobsmacked by seeing Gen in full Dr. Broussard mode.

"You listen to Genevieve," Mum said, looking as though she couldn't decide whether to hug Dad or smack him. "Tell her what she wants to know."

Then, and only then, did Dad admit to intermittent discomfort below his diaphragm. "Not pain, though, just an achy feeling."

"We're taking you to the hospital," Gen told him, and her no-nonsense tone left no room for discussion. "Zach, I don't want your father walking back down to the car, so call an ambulance, please."

He'd been so caught up in what was happening, he hadn't thought to do so and was kicking himself for that as he got up and stepped to one side to make the call. By the time he'd explained where they were and got the ambulance dispatched, Gen had come to stand beside him.

"They're on their way," he told her, suddenly realizing he felt unsteady, as though his head was about to float off his body. She put her hand on his arm, and the warmth of it steadied him, although there was nothing anyone could do to decrease his anxiety. He lowered his voice so it wouldn't carry to where his mum and dad sat. "Heart attack?"

She rubbed the back of her neck. "Could be, but I can't make a definitive diagnosis here. Once we get him to the hospital, we'll have a far better chance of getting to the bottom of it."

He looked over at his parents, saw the fear in his mother's eyes, even as she tried to keep a stiff upper lip, and his father's bravado as he attempted to look as though nothing out of the ordinary was happening.

"We'll take care of him, Zach." Gen sounded brisk. The voice of a woman in complete control. "Maybe you should go down to the road and make sure they know where to find us."

Not wanting to leave, he hesitated, but she put her hand on his cheek, and when he looked at her she gave him a soft, reassuring smile.

"I'll be here, keeping an eagle eye on him. Go on. The longer it takes them to find us, the longer it will be before we can figure out what's going on with your dad."

She was right, of course she was, but it didn't make it any easier. And not even the kiss she gave his cheek helped. Only the little shove on his shoulder finally got him moving, and he sprinted down the path, his ears straining for the sound of the siren coming in the distance.

He should have known something wasn't right with Dad since that first night when he was rubbing his chest and complaining about indigestion. As a nurse, he'd seen too many people die who'd assumed what they were experiencing could be cured with antacids, when they were, in reality, having a heart attack.

But he'd been too wrapped up in Gen, in the charade they were playing and his growing feelings for her. Too busy trying to guard his heart and his ego from being smashed again to pay proper attention to what was happening with his father.

Guilt racked him, as he looked back up the hillside, although the group was out of view.

This was the wake-up call he needed.

He'd been angry when Gen said she was going to confess to her mother. Not just because it meant what was going on between them would be over, but because he dreaded being embarrassed in front of his parents when it came out their relationship was a sham.

Dad and Mum had seemed so happy, even relieved, that he'd found someone. He hadn't wanted them to look at him the way they had after Moira's defection: with worry, and worse, pity.

Yet, none of that mattered now.

The only thing of importance was Dad's health, and keeping his mum on an even keel while they figured out what was happening.

"Thank God," he muttered as he heard the approaching siren and strained to see the ambulance turning into the gardens.

Then he was waving like a crazy man to get their attention, putting everything else aside in the push to help his father.

CHAPTER SEVENTEEN

GEN RODE IN the ambulance with Mr. Lewin, monitoring his vitals along the way. Ambulances in St. Eustace weren't the fully equipped conveyances she was used to. In fact, they were fairly basic, with a gurney that locked into place and a minimum of medical supplies, mostly just what was needed to staunch bleeding and administer oxygen.

Since Mr. Lewin was still suffering some shortness of breath, she put him on oxygen and used the BP monitoring system to track his blood pressure. She also took the opportunity to examine him more fully and ask additional questions, which he seemed more willing to answer when the rest of his family weren't present.

When they got to the hospital, she reluctantly handed Mr. Lewin over to Dr. Carmichael, the ER doctor on duty, but gave him her considered opinion before he went into the examination room.

"Blood tests will tell if he's had a series of mild myocardial infarctions," he said. "But I'll schedule him for the ultrasound, as you recommend."

She had to be content with that, but as she made her way to the waiting room, her worries about Mr. Lewin's condition stalked her along the corridor. Stopping at the nursing supervisor's office, she inquired which surgeons were on duty that afternoon.

"Dr. Cutler is here on-site," she was told. "And Dr. Langdon is on call."

"What about Dr. Goulding?"

"He's gone to Jamaica to attend an orthopedics conference and won't be back for another two days."

"And who's in charge in radiology?"

"Dr. Figueroa."

"Thank you," she said, now more worried than before.

If Mr. Lewin needed surgery, of the two options available her choice would be Kiah. But he was too close to Mr. Lewin for him to undertake the task. Omar Cutler was young and quite inexperienced. Gen had also found him far too cocky for comfort, not wanting to take advice or direction. Depending on the diagnosis, he might never even have performed the necessary procedure, but probably wouldn't hesitate to do it anyway.

At least Dr. Figueroa was head of radiology, so if he were needed, that aspect of the situation was covered.

When she walked into the waiting room, Mrs. Lewin got to her feet, her hand over her heart.

"It's okay," Gen said, going to hug her. "They're examining him now and will come and tell us when they have something to report."

"I thought you'd be looking after Hezekiah," she told Gen.

"She's a surgeon, Mum, and not even on duty right now. But don't worry. Dr. Carmichael is a good diagnostician."

"He really is," Gen agreed. "We just need to give him some time to do his job."

So they waited, and Gen could see Zach's anxiety level rising, although anyone else looking at him would think he was calm. She saw it in the way his fingers clenched and seemed to have to be forced to relax, and in the periodic joggling of his leg as his pent-up energy sought release.

It was long past lunchtime, and Gen started worrying about her mom, who'd been recently diagnosed with prediabetes, having something to eat. Yet, she was loath to leave Mrs. Lewin, wanting to be there in case she could be of help.

Finally, thinking it might do Zach good to have something to do, she asked if he'd take her mother to get some food and suggested he bring something back for his mom too.

He started to object, but his mother, who'd been all but silent, said, "That's a bonny idea, Zach. Gen can keep me company until you come back."

Her tone was such he didn't dare argue, so, with obvious reluctance and the demand that they call him right away if they got any news, he left.

As soon as it was clear he and Mom were probably out of the hospital, Mrs. Lewin said, "You know what's wrong with Hezekiah, don't you?"

Gen bit her lower lip, and then admitted, "I think I have a pretty good idea, but the tests will tell if I'm right or not."

"Will he need an operation—if you're right?"

"He will need surgical intervention, if I'm right." That was the most she was willing to say.

"And this…surgical intervention, is it something you can do?"

"I wouldn't be the best choice," she admitted. "But unfortunately, they don't have the type of specialist who would usually perform the surgery on staff here right now."

"But you can do it?"

Mrs. Lewin was unrelenting, and Gen reluctantly nodded. "I've done a few, but…"

The older lady's hand on her arm stopped her from continuing.

"If Hezekiah needs the operation, I want you to do it. I know he'd want that too."

"I can't promise, Mrs. Lewin. It might not be up to me."

That got her a shake of the head. "I know that if you put your mind to it, you'll find a way."

Then the other woman changed the subject, asking if Gen could call Zach and ask him to go to the house and get her knitting. Stepping out of the room, Gen wandered just outside the outer doors, wanting a breath of air, but staying where she could watch the entrance to the waiting area.

"Hey," she said when he answered. "No word yet, but your mom is wondering if you'd stop by the house and get her knitting for her."

"I can," he said. "But I want to be there when they tell us what's happening with Dad."

"I know," she replied, her heart aching for him.

Then he sighed. "At least you're there with her."

"It won't take too long to get what she wants," she said, trying to reassure him. "And it'll keep her hands occupied, hopefully calming her down some."

"Okay. We've got food, and I'm heading to the house, so I should be there in about twenty-five minutes or so."

"All right. Bye."

Hanging up, she stayed where she was for a while longer, contemplating what Mrs. Lewin had asked of her.

It could be tricky, getting the powers that be to agree to her operating on Zach's father, simply because they'd done such a good job of convincing everyone she and Zach were a couple. But if it were at all possible, she'd do it.

For Mrs. Lewin, and for Zach.

She couldn't allow doubt to cloud her mind, but she'd have to be superhuman not to realize whatever she and Zach had would shatter into ten thousand pieces if she operated unsuccessfully on his father.

"Coo-calloo-calloo," she muttered, but not even her favorite curse word was sufficient.

When Zach and Mrs. Broussard got back to the hospital, it was just in time to hear what Felix Carmichael had to say.

"Your husband has an abdominal aortic aneurysm, Mrs. Lewin. That's an area in the wall of the main artery running through his belly that's become weak and is swollen, like a balloon."

Zach expected his mother to look to him for clarification, but instead, she looked at Gen, who nodded slightly.

"What can you do about it?" Mum asked, twisting her fingers together.

"Well, it measures just about six centimeters, and depending on some of the other test results, he should be a candidate for endovascular stent grafting. If the surgeon determines the endo-vascular surgery isn't the right choice, then he or she will want to do a conventional repair."

As Carmichael explained the different pro-cedures to his mother, Zach was watching Gen, who was pressing her knuckle into the side of her lip and staring out the window. When Felix finished, he asked Mum if she had any ques-tions.

"Which one will be best for Hezekiah?"

"The surgeon will have to make that determi-nation, Mrs. Lewin. There are a lot of variables to consider and to talk over with your husband before a decision is made."

After that, Mum went quiet, seeming not to have anything else she wanted to ask, but Gen did.

"EKG results look…?"

"Very good, actually."

"And will you do a stress test?"

"That will be up to the surgeon."

"And who that will be?"

"I contacted Kiah Langdon, but although he's on his way in, he said he'd be unable to do the surgery because of his close relationship with the patient. I have a call in to the director for his input before I hand the patient over to a surgeon."

Zach was going to interject and ask who else was available, and why it was taking so long for the decision to be made when Gen's mother touched his arm and pointed.

His mum was silently crying, looking down at her lap, probably in the hope no one would notice. Zach knelt beside her and hugged her, stroking her back and whispering reassurances. By the time she'd calmed down, both Felix and Gen were gone.

Leaving Mum with Mrs. Broussard, telling them he had some questions of his own for the doctor, he tried to find them, eventually hearing Gen's voice from one of the consulting rooms.

The door was ajar, and he was in time to hear her say, "…Two choices. You let me operate, or you fly Mr. Lewin to Trinidad for the surgery, and I wouldn't suggest the latter. Considering the swift onset of symptoms, the abdominal pain and the size of the aneurysm, if you delay the surgery you're risking rupture. And you don't want that to happen at twenty thousand feet."

It sounded as though she were in battle mode, and Zach was about to knock and join the war when he heard another voice—that of Omar Cutler—and paused.

"I'm the surgeon on duty, so it's my responsibility to do the surgery."

"It would be your responsibility *if* you were assigned the case and were qualified to perform the procedure."

"I am qualified…"

"How many endovascular repairs have you performed? How many conventional open repairs?"

"I've assisted on…"

"Assisted isn't doing." Her voice was cold, cutting. "How many have you *done*, yourself?"

"Listen, don't get up on your high horse with me." The anger in the young doctor's voice was patently clear. "You can't do the surgery because you're sleeping with the patient's son, and it would be an ethical violation. Everyone knows it, so don't try to deny it."

"What does that have to do with anything?" Gen's voice was amused, dismissive. "Whatever Zach and I have going on isn't serious enough or important enough to make any difference.

And, as for the patient, I've only known him for a few days. There's no attachment there either."

No attachment there either?

Zach stepped back from the door, hearing the rise and fall of the continuing argument coming from behind it, but no longer listening.

...isn't serious enough or important enough to make any difference.

Him. She was talking about him, and the words cut through him like her scalpel.

Turning on his heel, he walked away.

Was this how boxers felt when they left the ring after a knockout? As though their brains had been scrambled, and nothing made sense anymore?

He'd told himself whatever there was between he and Gen didn't matter in the grand scheme of things, but hearing her dismiss him so easily, so *casually*, gave lie to that idea.

Somewhere, deep inside, he'd held on to some stupid hope that they might, just might, become a real couple. That she would realize she felt as deeply for him as he did for her and want to make a go of it.

He'd known better, faced the disparity in their lives and expectations and reminded himself she was out of his league over and over, but that hadn't stopped his stupid heart from getting involved.

Yet, wasn't it better to hear it like this, than to have her spell it out at a later date?

No. That was a lie too. No matter how he heard it, the grinding agony, the heartbreak, would be the same.

It was too much to deal with, and the part of his brain that controlled emotion, that was screaming with agony, shut itself down, recognizing his priorities.

Making sure Dad got the best treatment.

Holding Mum together as she watched her husband of almost forty years undergo a potentially dangerous surgery to repair a defect that could, if left alone, kill him.

It wasn't the first time he'd had to lock shame and anger away, to pretend everything was fine and make it through from one day to the next.

He'd done it before and come out on the other side, and he could, he *would*, do it again.

"Zach." Kiah's voice came from behind him, and Zach squared his shoulders, put on a mask of impassivity to greet his cousin. Kiah grabbed him and hugged him hard. "Man, why you never call me right away?"

"It all happened so quickly." How could his voice sound so normal, when his entire face, even his lips, felt numb? "And then…" He shrugged, at a loss to explain.

"I get it. I really do. What's happening now? Have you been in to see Uncle yet?"

"Not yet. I was just going to find out if I could take Mum in to see him."

"Come on," Kiah said, slapping him on the back. "I know one or two people around here, so I think I can get you past the guards."

Zach felt his lips curl, although of their own volition, and knew he'd survive it all intact.

Or as intact as a man with a shattered heart could be.

CHAPTER EIGHTEEN

GEN GOT HER WAY. Director Hamilton gave her the go-ahead to perform the surgery, but she knew now, more than ever before, she was under intense scrutiny.

Especially from Zach, who, from one instant to the next, had turned into a cold, somehow forbidding stranger, making her wonder if he doubted her ability to perform the operation.

Yet, they'd worked together so many times, surely he knew her well enough to realize she'd never endanger his father's life? That if she thought it was best for his father, she'd medically evacuate him to Port of Spain, where they had vascular surgeons on call?

The only people who were happy about the turn of events were Mr. and Mrs. Lewin.

When she'd gone in to see Mr. Lewin, who was yet to be transferred out of emerge, it was to find an almost party atmosphere in the room, mostly instigated by Kiah.

"Okay, everyone except Mrs. Lewin, out, please." She tried to catch Zach's eye, hoping to give him some kind of reassuring signal, but he avoided all eye contact and walked away without a word.

That was something to be dealt with later, she told herself, even though the slight hurt horribly.

"I knew you could do it, dear." Mrs. Lewin sent her a sweet, grateful smile, before explaining to her husband what she'd asked Gen to do.

He seemed equally appreciative. "Zach told us you're one of the best surgeons he's worked with, so I'm glad it'll be you working on me."

"Do you want Zach in here while I explain the differences in the procedures?"

They exchanged glances, and then Mr. Lewin shook his head. "No. I know you'll do right by me, and I don't want Zach involved. If anything were to go wrong, he'd blame himself."

Gen nodded, understanding and believing that to be true. Zach was exactly that type of man. The kind who would shoulder any burden for those he loved and take the blame if things went awry.

Just the type of man any woman with sense would love and want to have at her side for all of life's ups and downs.

But now wasn't the time to consider why

knowing that caused her heart to ache. She had an important job to do.

One that she was determined to succeed at—for all their sakes.

Having gone through Mr. Lewin's test results and looked at his scans, she told the older couple what she'd found.

"Either surgical option will work for you, and I checked to make sure that both are approved back in the UK, so follow-up shouldn't be a problem."

After she'd explained the advantages and drawbacks of the procedures, Mr. Lewin decided on the endovascular repair, mainly because of the quicker recovery time.

"I don't mind that I'll have to get regular checks to make sure it's still in place. I don't want to be laid up for weeks recovering from surgery if I don't have to be."

He'd been a bit upset when she told him she was admitting him to the hospital rather than sending him home, but she didn't sugarcoat it.

"From everything you've told me, and from what I've seen in your scans, this is a fast-growing aneurysm, and I don't want to take any chances on a rupture. Keeping you here, instead of having you go home, is just my way of making sure the chances are minimized, and also that if a rupture should occur overnight, you can get immediate care. Not that I think that will happen," she hastened to add when Mrs. Lewin's eyes widened. "I'm just being extra cautious."

She scheduled the surgery for midmorning the following day, after consulting with the Chief of Radiology to make sure he was available and ordering the necessary CT scan for that evening.

Then, she went looking for Zach and her mom, only to find Mom had driven herself back to Gen's place while Gen had been talking to his parents.

"We got your car at the same time I picked up Mum's knitting, and it didn't make sense for her to have to stay here waiting for you when we didn't know how long you'd be."

His words were innocuous, even polite, but the tone was cold enough to make her shiver. Then she remembered his anger earlier and decided now wasn't the time to get into any of it. Not with his dad about to have surgery, which she was going to perform.

No, best to let things ride and deal with it afterward.

If he were willing.

"Would you mind taking me home, then?" she asked. "Although I can take a cab, if you want to stay with your dad until visiting hours are over. They should be moving him to a room soon."

"No, I'll run you home," he said. "I just need to let Mum know I'll be back in a mo."

There it was again. Perfect courtesy, wrapped in a block of ice.

The drive to her place passed in silence broken only by the radio.

When they got to her condo, she took a leaf from his book, and said, "Thank you. No need for you to get out. I'll see you in the morning."

Then, with all the dignity she could muster, she got out of the car and walked up the path.

Her mom was in the living room watching TV when she got inside, and Gen's stomach rumbled at the smell of food emanating from the kitchen.

"I knew you were the only one who hadn't eaten," Mom said. "So I came back to put something together for you."

Gen showered and ate, keeping the conversation light. Her overwhelming need to come clean to her mother had faded, both in light of Mr. Lewin's illness and the confusion over Zach's behavior.

If he continued to treat her that way, there'd be no need to tell Mom anything. She'd be able to see for herself that the relationship had imploded.

"I'm sorry part of one of your last days will be spent by yourself, Mom. I'm going to sleep at the hospital tonight, just in case Mr. Lewin's aneurysm ruptures, and then I'm operating in the morning. Once I'm sure he's out of the woods, I'll come home, and we can do something together."

Mom just smiled. "I'll be fine. Do what you need to."

Gen called to make sure Zach and his mother had left for the night before she drove back to the hospital, not wanting another frosty encounter with her patient's son. Putting her bags down in the doctor's lounge, she went up to check on Mr. Lewin, finding him still awake and sitting up in bed.

He looked surprised when he saw her.

"I though Zach said you'd gone home."

"I did. But then I came back," she said casually, picking up his chart and looking at the notations.

"Well, I'm glad you did," he replied. "I wanted to talk to you alone, and wasn't sure I'd get the chance before the surgery."

Smiling, she put down the chart and walked over to the side of the bed.

"What did you want to talk about?"

He hesitated for a moment and then said, "I know you said the surgery tomorrow shouldn't be dangerous, but hearing you have a bomb in your belly waiting to explode makes a man think."

She held up her hand. "Don't start getting maudlin on me, sir, and talking about dying."

"No, no." He shook his head. "I trust you to make sure I get through okay, but, as my good friend from Jamaica always says, 'Any card can play.' No one knows what tomorrow will bring, so I wanted to tell you now—if anything does happen to me, take good care of Zachary. He's a good, good man, and he deserves to be happy, especially after what Moira did to him."

He said the name as though she should know who he was talking about, and she had to bite her cheek not to ask who that was and what she'd done. To do so would alert Mr. Lewin to the fact he'd said something he probably shouldn't have, and she didn't want him upset in any way.

So, instead of letting any of the questions flying around her head out of her mouth, she smiled and said, "I'll do the best I can, but you'll darn well be around to see it as long as I have any say in the matter, that is."

Later, lying on a cot in the doctor's rest room, trying to relax enough to sleep, she realized she didn't really care who Moira was. Although knowing the story would help her understand

Zach better, the most important question of all was: had he gotten over this Moira woman, or was there no place in his heart for anyone else?

Someone like her?

Despite the heat of their passion and the honest emotional connection she felt to him, was she just kidding herself to even think he'd want to be with her long-term? His recent coldness seemed to say she was, especially since she couldn't figure out why he'd suddenly seemed to turn completely away.

The sensation of being rejected brought back harsh, painful memories. It had happened before, in the most devastating of ways, and she knew the damage lingered, even now. Was that what she was facing again? Should she try to pursue a lasting relationship with Zach? Was she willing to open herself up to that type of pain again?

Yet, she couldn't get away from the fact that lying there in the dark, all she longed for was his arms around her, his voice in her ear. Zach had always made her feel safe, accepted and wanted, even though he knew she hadn't been completely open and honest with him about her past.

Now she faced the trap she'd set for herself.

If she told him about Johan and what had happened after the breakup, would he view the story as her trying to guilt him into giving their relationship a chance?

And if she didn't tell him—keeping her shame to herself, protecting her ego—would he think her reticence a sign that she didn't trust and love him?

Heart heavy and eyes damp, Gen called on years of discipline and closed her eyes, starting the relaxation technique she'd mastered to help her sleep on the worst of nights.

Mr. Lewin and all his family deserved to have her very best self in the OR in the morning.

Everything else, no matter how important to her, would have to wait to find resolution.

Zach made sure to take his mum to the hospital early enough to see his father before the surgery, and they found him in good spirits, although Zach wasn't sure if that was just an act for Mum's sake.

"There's mi darlin'," he said, with that cheeky look he reserved just for her, and they held hands until Nurse Monroe came to kick them out to prep Dad for the operation.

Gen had already been in and out of the room several times, once with Dr. Figueroa, and another time with the anesthesiologist. Mum had greeted her as though she were one of her children, but besides a brief "good morning," Gen and he hardly exchanged a word.

When the nurse told them it was time to go, there was a round of kisses and hugs, but after Mum stepped out, Dad called Zach back and asked the nurse for a moment with "his boy."

"Some 'boy,'" Nurse Monroe teased, looking at her watch and heading for the door. "You can have five minutes, but no more. Dr. Broussard is always punctual to the second."

"Zachary, your Gen tells me I'm going to pull through this and be fine, but if I don't—"

"Dad—"

His father held up his hand. "Son, nothing in life is certain, so I want you to know I love you, and I'm prouder of you than I can ever say. You're a fine, accomplished man, and I know I don't tell you that often enough, so I wanted to make sure I said it now."

"Okay, Dad." And although he tried to make his voice impatient, he knew he'd failed and that his father saw the tears gather in his eyes. "I love you too."

"Don't be afraid of love, Zachary," his father said, seemingly out of the blue. "I know it hasn't always been kind to you, but I think you've found something special now. Something like what Mum and I have. You should hold on to it, you hear?"

Before he could answer, Nurse Monroe was back, saying, "That's it, Zachary Lewin. Out. Unless you want the job of prepping your own daddy for surgery."

It was a long morning. Sitting in the waiting room outside the theatre wing gave him more than enough time to think all kinds of horrible, crazy thoughts.

Dad had opted for general anesthetic instead of an epidural. Suppose they gave him the wrong dosage or he was allergic? He wanted to ask Mum if Dad had ever had an operation before, but she looked so peaceful, sitting there with her knitting, that he didn't want her to start worrying.

What if the stent was the wrong size, or Gen tore the artery, or it ruptured before they could get the stent in place, or…or…or…

Realizing he was starting to go a little insane, he got up.

"Mum, I'm going to nip down to the canteen for a cuppa. Do you want one?"

"Yes, thank you, dear."

He was heading for the stairs when he saw Mrs. Broussard coming toward him carrying a beverage tray with cups in one hand and a paper bag in the other.

"Morning. I brought you and your mom some

tea and pastries. I know you probably wouldn't want a full breakfast or might have already eaten."

Taking the tray from her hand, he bent to kiss her cheek. "You're a lifesaver. I was just going down to get tea."

She smiled slightly, then sobered. "Any news?"

"Not yet. It'll be a little while yet, I think."

"Did you see ViVi at all this morning?"

"I did." He opened the door with his hip and held it for her to precede him into the waiting room.

"I hope she got some sleep. She always complained during her residency that the cots in the hospital were so terribly uncomfortable, and I doubt the ones here are any better. Ah, Sheila, how are you doing?"

As the women greeted each other, Zach let the fact that Gen had slept at the hospital sink in.

"Doing well, thank you," Mum said, accepting Mrs. Broussard's hug and returning it in kind. "I know Hezekiah is in good hands. Our Gen will take care of him."

Our Gen.

Mum said it as though Gen was one of her children, and Mrs. Broussard was smiling and nodding, as though it was quite fine with her too. Coupled with his father's advice the night before, Zach came to the inescapable conclusion that, like him, his parents had fallen head over heels for Gen.

It was a shame all of them were going to be disappointed when things fell apart.

Still restless, and unwilling to sit there and listen to the two ladies sing Gen's praises, he put the tray of drinks on the table, and said to them, "I'm going to walk around a bit."

His phone pinged as he left the waiting room and paced closer to the doors leading to the operating theatres. It was his sister, texting to ask for an update. He sent her a reply, saying Dad was still in the OR, and paced back the other way along the corridor again.

Ping.

The blasted phone again. He wanted to throw it against the nearest wall, even while acknowledging his role as the family's point of contact. Just as he got to the other end of the corridor and was reaching to take the phone out of his pocket, he heard the door to the operating wing open, and he spun on his heel.

Gen came through with Chief of Radiology Dr. Figueroa beside her, the two speaking in low voices, the radiologist shaking his head. Gen had her head down as she pulled off her surgical cap, and then she rubbed at the back of her neck.

240 ISLAND FLING WITH THE SURGEON

Zach was frozen in place, watching them come toward him, ice slipping and sliding through his veins, filling his belly. He couldn't read their postures. Couldn't even seem to think or reason.

Then Gen looked up and saw him, and the most beautiful smile he'd ever seen spread across her face.

"It went perfectly," Dr. Figueroa said, grinning too, as they got to his position. "Picture-perfect."

"Thank you," Zach said, but he only had eyes for Gen and her smile, which made all his previous anger, doubts and fears seem irrelevant.

He wanted to hold her, to take strength from her, find solace in her arms. And that rush of need was almost as terrifying as sitting in the waiting room while Dad had his operation.

"Let's go tell your mother," she said, putting her hand on his arm. At the tenderness of her touch, his legs, which moments before had threatened to give out, regained sensation.

As though struck by a bolt from the blue, he knew—acknowledged—that he'd never be complete without her in his life. That the emotions he'd fought so hard could no longer be denied and the warmth rushing through him, heating every muscle and sinew, was love.

Plain and simple.

But there was no benefit to telling her how he felt, no future stretching ahead of them. So all he said was, "Yes. Let's go."

Hiding this new pain, so no one would see.

CHAPTER NINETEEN

MR. LEWIN WAS ambulatory by the day following the operation and back up at the farmhouse that evening. Gen monitored him in the hospital and kept in touch with Zach once he was released, but most of the time was spent with her mother.

They went up to visit with the Lewins on the day of Mom's flight, and watching the older folks, Gen realized a real bond had been formed between the three of them. There were addresses exchanged and promises to keep in touch and open invitations to visit extended. Zach was quiet through it all, not contributing much to the conversation, busying himself with drinks and food, and making sure his Dad was comfortable.

To Gen, the way he avoided touching her was marked, but if any of the parents noticed, they were too polite to say.

"We've extended our trip by four days," Mrs. Lewin told them. "And then Zachary will fly with us to Port of Spain so we have someone to help with luggage and Dad's wheelchair. Then Cameron will meet us at Heathrow and drive us home."

"I wanted to just convalesce here," Mr. Lewin said, giving his wife a baleful glance from the corner of his eye. "But she decided she wanted to go home."

"I want him to be seen by our family doctor, so she knows what's happening," his wife interjected. "And besides, I've had enough of this heat."

Amused at their banter, Gen looked at Zach and found him staring at her in a way that made her insides melt. But as soon as their gazes clashed, he turned away and her heart sank. Seeing the fondness with which Mom took her leave from Zach, kissing his cheek and whispering something to him, just increased her pain.

After she and her mother got back from the Lewins' house, they sat outside on the patio, enjoying a final glass of lemonade before Gen was to take her to the airport.

"What's happening between you and Zachary?" Mom asked abruptly when there was a lull in the conversation. "I know you said the relationship was going slowly, because of his past experiences, but seeing you two together, I thought things were going well, until recently."

She'd shelved the idea of confessing the lies to her mom, and Gen had no intention of going back on that decision now, so she replied, "I'm really not sure, Mom. He just…went cold on me, but he's had so much on his plate, it's not surprising, is it?"

Her mother took a sip from her glass, seemingly lost in contemplation for a moment or two. Then she sighed.

"Did he tell you what happened to him in his last relationship?"

"With Moira?"

It was a calculated stab in the dark, but it hit home.

"Yes. That was her name."

"Not in a lot of detail."

Mom slid her a shrewd glance. "And have you told him about Johan and Loren and what you went through?"

Oh, she felt the trap then, but figured she might get away with the same prevarication she'd used before. "Not in a lot of detail."

Mom snorted and shook her head. "So, neither of you have told the other about the pain you carry and the fears you must have about going into another relationship. Baby, without trust, the relationship will never work. So, if you can't see your way clear to move forward in honesty, it's best you don't see each other anymore."

Those words stayed with her long after she'd dropped her mother off at the airport that evening.

Mom was right, of course, and Zach had said it too. Gen hadn't had the courage to be honest with him, afraid to open herself up to disdain or ridicule.

Afraid to trust again and have that trust thrown back in her face.

But was he that type of man? Could she see him doing what Johan had done?

Or was the fear a knee-jerk reaction on her part, an instinctive attempt to protect herself at all costs from something that felt so huge and important?

She couldn't decide, and in the face of her uncertainty, couldn't act. This was no longer a romp or a game, and the seriousness of it paralyzed her, forcing her to think rather than simply react, as she often did.

Hard enough to admit to herself she loved Zach, much less to consider admitting it to him and perhaps have him laugh. After all, hadn't he warned her not to get attached, and she'd agreed? It wasn't his fault she couldn't keep up her end of the bargain, and she didn't think he'd even want to know how she felt about him.

Yet, there was a part of her pushing to do something, anything, to come to a decision. Zach was, as his father had said, a good man—and kind too. Even though she internally cringed at the thought of his possible rejection, did she really think he'd be cruel?

No.

That wasn't the type of man he was.

And wasn't he worth risking everything—her ego, her heart—for?

He was, if she could just find the courage to be honest.

Still racked with hesitancy, as well as feeling ineffably lonely and needing something to do, she went up to the guest room and stripped the bed. Gathering up the sheets, along with the towels her mom had used, she carried them downstairs just as her doorbell rang.

When she looked through the peephole and saw Zach standing there, her heart flipped and her mouth went dry. Shoving the dirty linens under the hall console table, she opened the door, plastering one of her best and brightest smiles on her face, although it felt as if it would crack her skin wide open.

"Hi." He looked so stern, it took everything she had to speak and keep her smile in place. "What's up?"

"I have to ask you something. When you were

talking to Carmichael, before you were assigned Dad's surgery, was what I heard you say the truth?"

"I don't remember what I said, Zach." And she really didn't. All she remembered was her promise to his mother and being determined to keep it. "Do you want to come inside?"

He rubbed his hand across the top of his head, his narrowed gaze never leaving hers, and didn't respond to her offer for him to come in, and just said, "You told them what was happening between us wasn't important, and there was no *attachment* to me. Was that true?"

She stepped back, hanging on to the door, realizing this was it, the moment she had to decide whether to trust him or to let him go without him knowing she loved him and wanted him for her own.

"It wasn't," she admitted. "I'd made a promise to your mother to be the one to operate on your dad, and I knew I was the best person out of the surgeons available. I honestly don't even remember saying those things. I just remember being determined not to let your mom down and trying to make myself the obvious choice. I couldn't let my feelings for you get in the way."

He stepped through the doorway so they were only a foot or so apart.

"What feelings?" His voice was gravelly and

demanding, and she had no intention of denying him an answer.

Yet, still she hesitated, realized she was pressing her knuckle into the side of her mouth when he captured her hand with his, and electricity zinged up her arm.

"I'm in love with you," she confessed, the words coming out soft and wobbly, revealing the vulnerability she couldn't hide anymore.

Then she couldn't continue speaking, even if she'd wanted to, because she was in his arms, and he was kissing her as though she were air, and he'd been drowning. That was how she felt too—alive again, when for the last couple of days she'd felt dead inside.

Zach kicked the door closed behind him, and Gen linked her arms around his neck, letting him know with the tightness of her embrace that she didn't ever want to let him go.

He drew back, just far enough that she could feel his breath rushing across her face. "I want you, Gen. But I want to sort this out between us, before we make love again. Every time I touch you, I fall a little deeper."

She shivered at the gravelly admission, but didn't release her grip.

"I want you to fall all the way, like I have," she told him. "You're all I want. All I could ever need. So make love with me. I've missed you so much."

And when she led him upstairs, Zach made no further objections.

Making love with Gen once more blew his mind, ecstasy heightened by their confessions of love.

Afterward, she lay curled against his side, her head on his chest, and they finally got around to unraveling each other's mysteries.

"The Bell's seemed like the beginning," she told him. "But truthfully, what finally happened had started a long, long time before."

His heart ached for her as she told him about the series of blows that came one after the other. Bell's palsy endangering her career, her fiancé's admission that he wasn't attracted to her anymore because of the nerve damage.

"The real kicker, though, came when I found out he'd got engaged to the woman I considered my best friend in the world. They livestreamed the engagement party, and Loren knew I'd be watching because she was the one who sent me the link."

"What a pair of bastards." Zach felt as if he could throttle them both if they were nearby.

Gen snorted. "That's one way to describe them. I was back at my apartment by then but…"

Her voice faltered, and he heard her take a deep breath. "I lost it. Thank goodness my sister was there with me and stopped me from destroying the place, and perhaps myself too. It just felt like the last humiliating straw, and I was sure my life was better off over. Dad wanted to send me to a psychiatric hospital, but Mom took me home instead and pretty much nursed me back to normal."

"I'm so sorry, love." He was sorry and livid and oh, so grateful. "I'm glad you didn't hurt yourself. I'm so thankful you're here now, with me."

She rolled over to rest her chin on the hand she had on his chest, bringing them face-to-face. Her gaze was searching, and he wondered what she was looking for.

Then she asked, "That doesn't scare you?"

Confused, he replied, "What doesn't scare me?"

"I had a mental breakdown, Zach. No one in my family even talks about it, out of shame or fear—I don't know which."

"Or maybe out of a desire not to hurt you by bringing it up?"

She blinked and pressed her knuckle into her lip.

"I guess that's a possibility too," she conceded.

"They're probably waiting for you to mention it first. And to answer your question, no, it doesn't scare me in the slightest. You were under immense stress, and worse, had been treated with the worst kind of emotional cruelty. I'd be more surprised if you were completely unaffected."

Her eyes filled with tears, and she placed a kiss right over his heart. "I told you Mom was worried because she thought I was suffering the aftereffects of the Bell's, but it was all the other things that she was concerned about. My mental and emotional health, and the way I'd lost my ability to trust and wasn't sure I'd ever get it back again."

"I'll earn your trust, every day, until you have no more doubts," he vowed, using his finger to wipe away her tears.

Then it was his turn, but Gen forestalled him, saying, "You don't have to tell me about Moira tonight if you'd rather wait. Just tell me you've gotten over her, so you have space for me in your heart."

"My heart belongs to you," he told her honestly. "But I'd rather just tell you now, so we can move on."

Talking about it didn't hurt anymore. It still

stung, but it was a muted pain and only residual anger.

At least on his part.

Gen bounced up to sit cross-legged beside his hip, scowling more ferociously than he'd ever seen her do before.

With narrowed eyes, she said, "She dumped you, after ten years of you supporting her so she could go to law school? After you gave up your own ambitions to help her achieve hers?"

He shrugged. "That about sums it up."

"Wow. Talk about trust issues. Yours must be pretty serious too."

He contemplated her words. "Yes, but different. Moira thought she was better than me, because she came from a middle-class family who lived in a nice village, and I was born and raised in South London. She was always trying to 'improve' me, making it clear I wasn't good enough the way I was. When you and I met, I convinced myself you'd never be interested in me long-term because we come from two different worlds."

Gen shrugged. "You heard my mom talking about her grandmother, and my dad is only where he is today because he's smarter than should be legal, and had mentors who guided him in the right way. Sure, we're affluent, but it doesn't make us stuck-up, because we know where our roots lie."

"Not everyone stays grounded that way," he said, before telling her what Moira had said before she left, about being embarrassed by him.

Gen literally slammed her fist into her other palm as she listened, clearly livid.

Zach found himself fighting back laughter, and she turned that furious gaze on him.

"How can you laugh, Zachary? You're the finest, most wonderful man I've ever met, and she has the nerve to say something like that to you? I want to grind her into pieces right now."

In between chuckles he told her, "I've never seen anyone do the Hulk smash into their own hand in real life. It was cute."

"Cute?"

She was trying for outrage, but amusement was getting the better of her, and he couldn't resist tugging her back down, then rolling so he was above her, and they were face-to-face.

"Incredibly cute," he teased, feeling light and free in a way he couldn't remember ever experiencing before. "Like kitten cute."

"You better stop while you're ahead, Zachary Lewin. Remember I wield a scalpel for a living."

But the threat lost most of its potency, her breathy voice betraying anything but anger.

"Tell me again," he demanded.

She knew exactly what he needed, as she lifted her head so her lips were soft against his.

"I love you, Zach. Just the way you are, and forever."

And that was all he needed to know.

* * * * *